KINDA LIKE BROTHERS

COE BOOTH

SCHOLASTIC INC.

 ▪ ISBN 978-0-545-78949-3

10 9 8 7 6 5 4 3 2   14 15 16 17 18

Printed in the U.S.A.   40

First printing, October 2014

The text type was set in Apollo MT.

Book design by Sharismar Rodriguez

• FOR HASAN •

SEPTEMBER 4, 1:05 A.M.

HE'S LEAVING.

Kevon.

He's in the corner of the room throwing stuff in that stupid army bag he got, trying to be real quiet. It's, like, after one o'clock in the morning, and he probably thinks I'm asleep. But I'm not. Never was. I'm wide awake, watching every move he makes.

Kevon starts looking around the room like maybe he forgot something. Real fast, I close my eyes so he won't see me spying on him, and I don't open them till I hear him leave the room.

And I'm, like, good.

He's gone.

If it was up to me, he would disappear and never come back.

ONE

IF THIS WAS A MOVIE, IT WOULD START THE NIGHT he got here, back at the beginning of August. I was trying to sleep when I heard, "Jarrett. Get up."

It was still the middle of the night, and I probably hadn't even been asleep for more than an hour. But my mom's voice was getting louder and louder.

"Jarrett, you have to get up."

I pulled the blanket over my face and tried to ignore her, but I should have known better. That never works with her. A few seconds later, she turned on the lights in my room, and it was so bright I couldn't even take it.

I flipped over on my stomach and pressed my head into the pillow to make it all go away, but that didn't stop her. "Jarrett, are you up? You have to wake up. The caseworker is going to be here soon, and I need you to help me get this room ready. Come on."

I let out a long, loud groan. She wasn't gonna leave. She wasn't. I didn't have a choice. I had to get up.

It wasn't till I had slowly slid down off the top bunk that I figured out she wasn't making any kinda sense. Get *this* room ready? *For what?*

While I stood there, not knowing what was going on, my mom was busy taking some of my magazines off the bottom bunk and putting them on the floor by the ugly, lopsided totem pole I made in fourth grade.

"Take all those dirty clothes off the chair and put them in the hamper." The way she looked around my room with her face all scrunched up, you would have thought it was covered in rotten bodies left over after a zombie invasion. "Lawd," she said, and her accent suddenly got thicker, so I knew she meant what she was about to say, "this room is shameful. And it stinks."

"It's not that bad," I said even though it really was kinda bad that day. Well, the whole year, really.

"Hurry." She pointed to the chair.

I grabbed all the clothes and started to walk outta my room, trying to make sure I didn't drop anything. Then I stopped at the door. "Wait a minute. What does *my* room have to do with anything?" I waited for her to answer me, but she didn't. She was too busy taking the sheets and everything off the bed.

I sighed real loud to get her attention. "If we're getting a baby, I don't think the caseworker is gonna care if my room is messed up or not."

Still no answer. So I stomped outta the room and into the bathroom to dump all my clothes in the hamper.

My mom takes in babies, most of the time in the middle of the night. She's a foster mother, and we get all kinda babies all the time. Sometimes they were abused or their parents didn't take good enough care of them or something. Most of the time they only stay with us for a little while, like a couple of days or weeks. Then they go somewhere else. We're just temporary.

What I didn't know was why my mom was putting me in the middle of it this time.

I went back to my room and stood there watching my mom fix everything up. "Can I just go back to sleep?" I asked. "I'm tired." It was exactly 12:36 in the morning. I went to bed around 10:00, but it took me a while to fall asleep. I couldn't stop thinking about everything that had happened that day, how I'd found out I was stupid. *Officially* stupid.

My mom finally looked at me. "You've been sulking around all day, Jarrett. I know you're upset, but —"

"I'm wasting my whole summer!" I said, and my voice got kinda loud, which made my mom raise her eyebrows at me.

"It's not a waste. You're learning a lot of new —"

"I'm not learning *anything*! And now that teacher doesn't even wanna let me —"

"You don't know that," Mom said. "You don't know what she and the principal were talking about."

"They were talking about *me*!"

"Well, you shouldn't have been spying on them. If you had been caught —"

"I wasn't caught," I said. "I'm never caught."

"That's enough, Jarrett," Mom said, throwing up her hands. "The caseworkers are on the way. We'll talk some more about this tomorrow."

I sighed as loud as I could. She was always doing that. Pushing me to the side for one of the babies. Nothing new about that. "Can you at least tell me what's going on? And can you tell me what this has to do with my room because I don't get this."

"The agency called and they're bringing over a baby," she said. "A little girl. She was injured this evening and those poor kids have been in the emergency room all night."

"There's more than one?"

"The baby has an older brother. That's why we need your extra bed."

"No way!" I said. "Why does he have to — ?"

"Calm down, Jarrett."

Easy for her to say. Why should I calm down? She wanted me to sleep in my room with some little kid I didn't know who was probably gonna cry all night and pee in the bed. "How old is this kid anyway?" I asked.

"He's twelve."

My mouth flew open. "He's *older* than *me*? That's not even fair!"

"Relax," she said, all calm, probably because some stranger wasn't gonna be sleeping in *her* room. "He's only going to be here for a day or two, until the agency can find a home that wants to take both kids and keep them together. The baby has special needs and —"

"I have special needs, too!" I practically shouted. "I *need* to have my own space and be left alone."

My mom didn't pay me any attention. She just took the rest of the stuff off my bottom bunk. "The agency is going to keep looking for a home for them. If we don't take them tonight, they're going to have to split them up."

None of that was my fault. She was just trying to make me feel guilty.

"Jarrett," she continued, "you know how hard it is finding a foster home that's willing to take older boys. It's a real problem. If we don't accept him, they'll probably put him in a group home."

Yeah, but that wasn't *my* problem.

My mom went outta the room and came back with some clean sheets even though the ones that were on there were already clean. My friend Ennis stayed over every Saturday night, but he'd been in Jamaica for the past three weeks and he wasn't coming back till Friday.

"He's just a normal boy your age," Mom said even though he probably wasn't. "Just see if he's interested in the same things you are. Maybe he's into those puppets, too."

"They're not puppets," I said. "They're *masks*. Horror masks."

"Well, maybe you two boys can play with the masks."

I sighed, even louder than before, louder than I thought was humanly possible. Did she think I was six years old or something? She wasn't listening to me, and it wasn't the first time.

But I knew nothing I said to her was gonna change what was about to happen. Not at all.

I was stuck.

TWO

WHEN MY ROOM WAS CLEAN ENOUGH FOR MY MOM, she went to the baby room because Abby, the foster baby we already had, started crying. That baby loved to cry. I stayed in my room for a while, sitting on my bottom bunk, stressing out.

Abby was in the baby rocker seat, still crying, when I got out to the kitchen. The microwave beeped and Mom took out the bottle, screwed on the nipple, poured a little on her wrist to see if it was too hot, then started feeding Abby. Finally, the baby stopped crying.

I had no other choice but to stand there and wait. So I got down the box of oatmeal raisin cookies and took two without asking. I needed them.

About twenty minutes later, while Mom was putting Abby back in her crib, the intercom rang. Since I was the only one in the kitchen, I had to buzz the caseworkers in.

"Mom!" I yelled. "They're here!"

She came down the hall. "If you wake that baby up, I swear —"

"Sorry. I was just —" I shook my head. "Forget it."

I didn't have time to argue. They were on the way upstairs. Times like that, I wished we lived in a big building, like, with forty-something floors. But we only lived on the top floor of a two-family house. I had, like, fifteen seconds, *tops*, before my space was invaded by some strange foster boy.

The doorbell rang and my mom went to answer it, leaving me in the kitchen looking stupid. One of the caseworkers came in first, carrying a little girl in her arms, wrapped in a yellow blanket. She wasn't a little newborn baby like Abby. She looked like she was, like, two years old, but I wasn't sure. The only thing I did know was that something really bad happened to her tonight.

She was asleep, but right there on her face, over her left eye, she had a giant white bandage. Even from where I was standing, I could still see there was blood trapped under it.

It was hard looking at her. I can't stand when we get babies that have casts or bandages on them. It makes me mad.

I was so busy looking at the baby, I didn't even notice the other kid till he was already in the apartment. He must have come inside behind the second caseworker because he was just standing there in the doorway looking at the floor till my mom said, "Come inside, sweetheart, and have a seat."

Mom, both of the caseworkers, the baby, and the boy walked into the living room, and, since he wasn't all hunched over looking at the floor anymore, the first thing I noticed was how tall he was. He wasn't a giant, but he was probably at least four inches taller than me.

None of this was fair. At all.

Then I got a good look at what he was wearing. Nothing special, really. Just a pair of blue no-name-brand sweatpants and a plain black T-shirt. But everything was way too big on him. It all looked new, too, even the sneakers he had on, some cheap sneakers that nobody in Newark would be caught dead wearing. He had a regular backpack on his shoulder, and he was carrying this huge army bag, like he was gonna be staying with us for months instead of just a couple of days.

The caseworker carrying the baby sat down on the couch and the other one sat next to her. Then the boy sat in one of the chairs on the other side of the room. He still didn't say anything, and I wasn't even sure if he saw me yet. I was staring at him though. I just wanted to figure out what he was thinking, what it must be like for him being in this apartment with people he never met before, knowing that in a little while the caseworkers were about to leave him here.

The only thing I could tell by looking at him was that he was tired. Real tired. And that made me think about what my mom said about them being through a lot tonight, and all I wanted to know was what happened to them. And who did it.

The kettle whistled and I turned it off before my mom could tell me to. Mom asked if any of the caseworkers wanted any tea and they both said no, they were okay. "What's your name, sweetheart?" my mom asked the boy.

"Kevon," he mumbled.

"I'm Ms. Ashby. Are you hungry? Would you like some juice?"

He shook his head.

The caseworker who wasn't holding the baby said, "He ate at the hospital. This boy can eat. He had two cheeseburgers." She smiled kinda weak at him, but he didn't smile back or anything.

The other caseworker handed the baby to my mom real careful, which was good because she didn't wake up. "We fed little Treasure earlier, too. The doctor gave her a tetanus shot, so she'll probably sleep through the night."

While Mom and the caseworkers talked about what kinda food the baby ate and all that, I just stood there quiet, trying to find out what happened. But they were only talking about boring stuff, so I ended up staring at Kevon. There didn't seem to be anything wrong with him except the fact that he was wearing sneakers like that.

One of the caseworkers put a folder on the table. "Here's some information about Treasure. As you'll see, she has a very long medical history. She's twenty-three months old, but she has some developmental delays and she hasn't started speaking yet. She had, uh, birth complications." She looked over at Kevon, but he was back to staring at the floor.

The caseworker gave my mom another folder. "This is some information on Kevon. He's in very good health, no allergies. The only concern is his teeth. Tonight he was seen by the emergency room dentist. She did some temporary work to help with the pain, but Kevon needs to follow up with a dentist as soon as possible."

"Okay, I'll call my dentist in the morning."

This kinda talk went on for a few more minutes till, for some reason, my mom remembered me and said to the caseworkers, "Oh, this is my son, Jarrett."

I half smiled and kinda waved. There were always caseworkers in my house, either dropping off babies or picking them up. I didn't think I ever met these two before, but I wasn't sure. They all start to look the same after a while.

I could tell my mom wanted to talk to the caseworkers by herself because all of a sudden she said, "Jarrett, take Kevon to your room and let him put his bag down." And then she flashed me a look, which I think was supposed to tell me not to ask Kevon any questions about why he got taken away and put with us.

"Okay," I said, not really feeling like going through with this. But there was no getting outta it.

So I started to walk down the hall, with him following me. And the truth was, he looked like he wanted to be there as much as I wanted him there.

Not at all.

THREE

WHEN WE GOT TO MY ROOM, I DIDN'T KNOW WHAT to do or say to Kevon, this foster kid who was older than me. Who was going to be sleeping in my room even though I didn't even know his last name. So I said the first thing that came to my mind. "Why did they take you away and put you here?"

He stood there and shrugged. "Long story."

I waited for him to start telling me the long story, but he didn't. He just looked around the room and asked, "Where am I supposed to put this?"

He was talking about the big bag he had over his shoulder. Now that I saw it up close, it looked really, really old. It could have been something from Vietnam or, like, the Civil War probably.

I pointed to the corner, to the trunk where me and Ennis kept our art supplies. "On top of that." There really wasn't anywhere else.

"What's up with your mom?" Kevon asked. "She cool or what?"

"Yeah, she's cool."

"Good. What kinda accent is that she got?"

"She's from Guyana," I said. "That's how they talk there." Not that I've ever been there or anything.

Kevon looked around the room, then stopped at my totem pole. "You made this?"

"No, I mean, yeah, but when I was little." Now that he was looking at it, I couldn't figure out why I still had that thing. I should have thrown that totem pole out years ago. It was embarrassing.

Good thing Kevon didn't say anything else. He just kept looking around. "These masks are nice."

"Thanks," I mumbled.

"You collect them or what?" He held up one of the Dumpster monster masks, the last one me and Ennis made before he left for Jamaica.

"No, not really. Me and my friend, we make them. We make trailers for horror movies." I knew I was making it all sound better than what it was. Our trailers weren't only low budget. They were *no* budget.

"Yeah? Movies? How you get into that?"

"Long story," I said, and I have to admit, saying that felt good.

He shook his head. "Alright. I hear you." He sat down on the bottom bed, and he looked more tired now than he did a little while ago. "How old are you anyway?" he asked me.

"Eleven." For a second, I thought about adding "and a half," even though I stopped doing that when I was six. I just wanted him to know he wasn't that much older than me.

But I ended up not saying anything else because it wasn't any of his business when my birthday was.

"You think they're done talking about me yet?" he asked.

I shrugged.

"Because I can't leave Treasure out there like that."

"My mom got her. She's okay."

"Treasure's not like every other baby. She's different. She's —"

"My mom knows how to take care of all babies. Some foster mothers don't, but my mom is good with babies that are, um, you know, special."

Kevon glared at me. "Well, Treasure doesn't know your mom. She knows me."

"I'll go see if they're done talking," I told him. "I'm real good at spying."

I slipped outta my room, not really feeling all that good about leaving him alone with my stuff. But I wanted to know more.

I crept down the hallway without making any noise at all. When I got close to the living room, I pressed my back against the wall and listened. Of course, they were in the middle of their conversation, and I could tell I missed most of the details because what I heard was one of the caseworkers say, ". . . tragic couple of years for this family. And now this."

"That's so sad," my mom said. "Poor kids."

What was so sad? I wished the caseworker would go back and repeat everything she had just told my mom. I needed facts.

Sometimes I could figure out why the babies who came to our apartment were taken away from wherever they were from, especially if they were abused and came to our house with bruises or a broken bone. Or if they were born addicted to drugs like Abby was, because those babies act different from other babies and cry a lot more. But I never got to know anything for sure about the other foster kids because my mom always told me it wasn't any of my business.

I heard the front door start to open, so I ran back down the hall, still trying to be as quiet as possible before I got caught. When I got back to my room, Kevon said, "So?"

"They're still talking," I said.

Now I could hear Terrence's deep voice from the living room.

"Who's that?" Kevon asked. "Your pops?"

"Nah, that's Terrence. Him and my mom go out. He's her boyfriend or whatever." I never knew what to call Terrence.

"And he comes over this late?"

"He works at the airport at night." Terrence's job was carrying all the suitcases on and off the planes, which looked like hard work, even for a guy with the kinda muscles Terrence had. "Sometimes they make him do overtime."

I decided it was time to go back out to the living room and Kevon followed me. Terrence sounded like he was in a real good mood by the way he was talking to the caseworkers. My mom was still holding Treasure, so Terrence showed the caseworkers around the apartment. They had to make sure we had food in the house for Kevon and Treasure, and that we had smoke detectors and window guards. Then he had to show them where Kevon and Treasure were gonna be sleeping. Every single caseworker that comes to our house has to do the same thing.

Finally, everybody came back down the hall and, as the caseworkers were leaving, Terrence told them to get home safe and all that. Then he closed and locked the door behind them.

That's when he finally said something to me and Kevon, who were still standing in the hall. "Hey, guys," he said. He shook Kevon's hand. "Terrence."

"Kevon."

Then he put his arm around my shoulder. "What's up, Jarrett? Why you still awake, man?"

"A lot going on," I said, eyeing Kevon real fast.

"I see that." He looked over at my mom on the couch, still holding Treasure, who was sleeping. "You boys need to go to bed. You gotta get up in the morning, Jarrett."

I told Terrence okay, but Kevon didn't move. "I need to put Treasure to bed," he said.

"You don't need to worry about that," Terrence told him. "She's in good hands."

It looked like Kevon was about to say something else, but he gave up, maybe because he was so tired. He turned around and slowly started walking down the hall back to my room.

I was walking real slow, too. Slow enough to hear Terrence say to my mom, "I thought we had an agreement, Kimma."

"They were going to split her up from her brother," she said. "I couldn't let that happen, not after what this little one went through today."

I heard Terrence sigh. There was something about my mom that made people sigh a lot around her.

I got to my bedroom where Kevon was already making himself comfortable on my bottom bunk. I still couldn't believe this was happening to me. But I couldn't avoid this forever. It was time to get this night over with already.

FOUR

WHEN I WOKE UP THAT NEXT MORNING, IT FELT like I didn't hardly get any sleep at all. For a couple of minutes, I didn't get outta bed. I just laid there trying not to move, because I didn't know if Kevon was awake and if he was, what was I supposed to say to him?

Then I heard a baby cry. From the bottom bunk bed. I leaned my head over the side of the top bunk and looked down. Kevon was sleeping, and right there, sitting up next to him was Treasure.

The baby cried for about thirty seconds before Kevon woke up. He sat up real fast and looked around like he didn't know where he was. I was still hanging over the bed watching the whole thing.

Kevon looked over at Treasure kinda mad and whispered to her, "You don't gotta cry all the time, Treasure. God, I'm right here."

I eased my head back over so he wouldn't see that I was spying on him. Yeah, it was my room and I could spy on whoever I wanted to here, but in a way it didn't feel like my own room anymore. There were two of them and only one of me. It kinda felt like *their* room and *I* was the intruder now.

Kevon kept talking to Treasure and I kept listening. I was thinking maybe he was gonna say something about what happened the night before, but he didn't say anything good. All he did was try to get Treasure to stop crying. "We're gonna go home," he told her. "In a couple days."

My mom came into the room. "Kevon? What — *why* is the baby in here?" She was mad, but she was trying not to sound it.

"She always sleeps in the bed with me," Kevon said. "It's nothing you need to worry about."

Mom glanced up at me, and me and her looked at each other for a couple seconds. She knew I was listening, but what did she expect? It was my room.

"How did she get in here?" Mom asked Kevon.

"I went in and got her. I didn't want her waking up in some strange place and start crying."

Mom didn't look all that happy about him going into the baby room. But what she said was, "I understand. But you don't have to worry about her, Kevon. I'm going to take good care of her."

"I don't mean nothing by it, Ms. Ashby, but you don't have to take care of Treasure. I been doing that forever, since she was born."

Personally, I didn't like the way he was talking to my mom, like he thought he was better than her. He didn't know that she'd been taking care of babies for a real long time, starting with me and never stopping.

"You've done a very good job taking care of her, Kevon, but

now that you're here, Treasure is my responsibility. And so are you. You can relax now."

Abby started crying from the baby room.

"Come here, Treasure," Mom said, reaching over and picking up the baby. "Let's go get Abby, and I'll pick out some clothes for you two pretty little girls."

As soon as Treasure was on my mom's hip, she stopped crying.

"Get dressed, Jarrett," Mom said. "You have to leave in an hour. Kevon, you don't have to get up right now."

"I'm up already."

"Okay, then. The caseworkers told me you didn't have any clean clothes except for what they gave you last night. So let's get all the dirty clothes out of your bag and into the washing machine. Jarrett will show you where it is."

Now she was volunteering me for everything.

She left the room with the baby, and when I looked down over the bed again, Kevon was sitting up with his arms folded in front of him, mad. He was staring at the door like he was waiting for my mom to come back and give Treasure back to him, but that wasn't gonna happen.

Kevon looked up at me. "What *you* want, Jared?"

"Nothing," I said. "And it's *Jarrett*, not Jared."

"She always like that?"

I didn't answer. It was one thing for me to complain about my mother, but who was this kid to do it? He should be happy my mom gave him a place to sleep last night. I jumped down off my bunk bed and said, "I have to get dressed." Then I left the room before he could say anything else.

When I was ready, I went into the kitchen. Treasure was in the high chair eating some oatmeal, and Mom was holding Abby, giving her a bottle. It was the only thing that stopped that baby from crying.

Mom made some toast and little slices of cheese for me. I used to be able to eat Cinnamon Toast Crunch and stuff like that, but Mom read some stupid article that said if kids ate sugar before school they wouldn't be able to concentrate. So for the whole time I'd been in summer school she made me eat twelve-grain bread and cheese, or eggs and turkey bacon. She said I couldn't eat anything that was white, which didn't make any sense because cereal wasn't even white. And I couldn't drink orange juice or apple juice because they were too sweet, but I could have plain milk, *which was white*.

Treasure was making a mess with oatmeal all over the place, but she was eating all the blueberries and banana slices my mom put on the tray. She was shoving them in her little mouth, chewing and smiling at the same time.

"Did you put on deodorant?" Mom asked me.

"Yeah."

"Go put on deodorant, Jarrett. You need to use it every day."

"Alright!" Why was she acting like that, like I stank or something? I went back to the bathroom and put on the stupid deodorant she bought for me. Then I came back to the table.

"It's going to be bad outside today," she said. My mom checked the weather every morning to find out if it was gonna be a bad day for asthma or not. "You have your inhaler?"

I didn't answer. I just nodded. She asked me the same things every single day. Did I put on deodorant? Did I have my inhaler? She was treating me like I was a kid or something.

"And don't walk to the Center. Take the bus. Don't spend too much time outside in the heat, okay?"

I nodded again. Maybe she couldn't help herself.

Before I even took the first bite, Mom said, "Hurry up. You don't want to miss the 8:10 bus."

I shook my head and said under my breath, "I don't wanna go."

"Well, you are."

"There's no reason to. I heard what Mrs. Greer said about me when she didn't know I was there. I know what she thinks about me."

"I told you a million times about spying on people." I knew Mom was just trying to change the subject. This wasn't about me spying on anybody. This was about my teacher telling the principal that I was too dumb to pass sixth grade, no matter what I did.

"Mom," I said, trying to explain it all to her again, so she would understand. "Mrs. Greer told the principal I was gonna fail. I heard it with my own ears. So why do I have to keep going to summer school?"

"She didn't say you were going to fail, Jarrett. She said you were struggling and —"

"You didn't hear her. *I* did. She said I was gonna have to do sixth grade all over again."

"I think she's looking out for you. She thinks if you repeat sixth grade, you'll understand the work better. You missed a lot of school last year because of your asthma. Maybe she thinks you need time to catch up and —"

"— and be the only one I know stuck in sixth grade when everybody else is in seventh, right?"

"She's not trying to punish you," Mom said. "And she's not saying you *can't* pass. Why don't you see how the rest of summer school goes? You still have almost two weeks left."

"It doesn't matter. She already made up her mind about me."

I ate as slow as I could, hardly even tasting anything.

Then Mom stood up and said, "I don't want to put this baby down and get her crying again. Hold her for a minute so I can go to the bathroom." She handed Abby to me real careful.

Sometimes I didn't understand my mom. First she told me I was gonna be late, and then she was telling me to sit there with a baby. Not that there was anything new about it. She always expected me to watch the babies when she had to go to the bathroom or something.

But that day I didn't care because I wasn't in the mood to go to school anyway. So I sat with Abby, and I let her grab my finger with her little baby hand, but just for a little while. After that, I took my finger away from her even though she still wanted it.

I wasn't trying to be mean or anything. I just didn't want her getting too attached to me. Then it would be hard for her when the caseworkers came and took her away from here. No, it was better for the babies if they didn't get too close to us.

FIVE

THE LAST THING I WANTED TO DO THAT DAY WAS go back to stupid summer school. First of all, I wasn't even going to my regular school. When they told me I had to go to summer school, Mom decided to sign me up at this charter school, the same one that hijacked the top floor of my school. Me and my friends hated the charter school, and we had a good reason to. Because of that school, we had to squish our whole school into two floors, and they cut our gym in half to share with them, which wasn't even fair.

Second of all, the name of the charter school was Central Boys Academy. There were no girls anywhere. Mom said she wanted me to try something different for the summer, and she liked the school because there were less kids in each class. But the real reason was, she thought I would concentrate better when girls aren't around.

Not true, by the way.

Another thing, the teachers there treated us like we were in the army or something. Everything had to be perfect all the time, and we had to say, "Yes, sir," and "Yes, ma'am," and all that.

When I walked into the classroom that morning, Mrs. Greer smiled all big and fake, but I wasn't buying it. I knew what she really thought of me. I had heard her tell Mr. Johnson that kids like me sometimes were better off repeating a grade.

So I didn't smile back at her. I just slid into my seat, not even looking at her. Nine more days. Then this whole stupid summer-school-for-boys nightmare would be over. Nine days to convince her I was ready to go to seventh grade with the rest of my friends.

It wasn't fair that people were counting me out, keeping me down, before I even had a chance to try.

▪ ▪ ▪

After school, I didn't feel like waiting for the bus, so I walked the ten long, hot blocks to the Center. On the way there, I passed a lot of little kids, running around, having fun. But not the kids my age. They were just standing around, doing nothing. If me and my friends didn't go to the Center, that was probably what we would be doing, just hanging out on the block. That's what a lot of teenagers do around here, too. Some of them don't even go to school. All night, I can hear them outside, acting stupid and sometimes getting in trouble with the police. It's like they don't have anything else to do.

My mom is always telling me I'm not gonna end up like them because she's gonna make sure I don't. But maybe those kids had mothers that tried to do the same thing, but it didn't work. Maybe those guys didn't do good in school either and that's why they stopped going.

That day, the Center was crazy. And loud. But it was like that every day. Everybody was running in and outta the rooms, but most of the noise was coming from the gym.

I looked up at the schedule to see what I was missing out on. They were having basketball practice in the gym. Me and Ennis had tried out for the team, but the whole thing was a joke. No way were they gonna put somebody short like me on the team. Ennis knew he would make it, but he said he would turn it down if they didn't pick me, too. They didn't.

I kept reading the schedule till I saw *Secret Project — Invited Guests Only*. Oh, man, I was late. I had already missed twenty-five minutes.

I practically ran down the hall to the room where everybody was meeting. The door was locked, and there was black construction paper covering the window on the door.

I knocked and waited. Finally, Qasim opened the door a crack. He's a college guy who only works at the Center in the summer. When he saw me, he said, "Get in here, man. You're late."

I slipped in and saw all the guys were already there, standing in two rows. And most of them were already sweating. "Sorry, man," I said, getting into my place in the second row. I hated being late, especially for step practice. I wasn't the best at it to begin with. Stupid summer school was messing me up on everything.

"Don't worry about it," Jess said. She was in college, too, but she worked at the Center all year and helped us with our homework after school. She was the only girl we allowed in the room because she was cool. And she was Qasim's girlfriend, so he probably couldn't tell her she had to leave.

Qasim was the one who got us into this whole thing. He's in a fraternity at college, and him and his frat brothers go around and compete in these step team competitions. He showed us some videos of them online and they're cool. Just a group of guys stomping on the floor and clapping and doing moves all together to a beat. Sometimes they did the moves holding canes. What I like about step is when you're doing it, you can't help but look strong. And tough.

So what we were gonna do was surprise the girls at the block party. All us guys were gonna get in the middle of the street and stomp and jump and clap and show the girls what real men looked like. And they were probably gonna be standing there screaming because that's what all the girls from Qasim's college did when the guys came out and did their step routine for them. I needed all the help I could get with girls. Especially one girl. The only one I ever thought about. The one I couldn't stop thinking about if I tried.

We got right into practice. In my head, I had to think out the steps. *Stomp left, stomp right, clap in front, clap behind my back, left knee up, clap under knee, stomp, right knee up, clap under knee, stomp, jump, clap in front, jump, clap behind my back.*

"Keep your steps tight, everybody," Qasim called out. "Move faster."

Faster? Was he crazy? I could barely keep up as it was.

There was a loud knock on the door. Qasim shook his head, and went over and opened the door a crack. All we heard were girls giggling from the other side of the door. "What are you doing in there?" one of them asked. I couldn't see who it was, and I didn't know the voice. Might have been this girl Milagros who's always kinda nosy.

"Yeah, why you have the door locked?" another girl asked.

Qasim blocked the door. "C'mon, girls," he said. "You know this is a private group. Go back to talking about shoes and skirts and lip gloss the way you girls like to do."

All of us guys laughed.

"Is that all you think girls talk about?" another girl asked, and when I heard that voice, I knew exactly who it was without even seeing her. It was Caprice. She was back from her family reunion in Atlanta. "Girls have more important things to do, you know, than just talk about clothes and makeup."

I tried not to smile, but it was hard.

Caprice was back.

■ ■ ■

By the time class was over, I was sweating, and it was kinda hard to catch my breath. But I wasn't about to pull out my inhaler in front of the other guys. It was bad enough that I kept messing up the step routine all the time. The last thing I needed was for everyone to know I had asthma, too. So I just leaned against the wall for a minute and tried to relax till my breathing got back to normal. Then I went back over to the other guys.

"Man, you suck," this thirteen-year-old guy José said to me. He slapped me on the back kinda hard, laughing, but not really at me. That's just the way he acted. But still, I didn't really wanna hear that.

This other guy Hector came up to him and said, "Don't mess with Jarrett, man. This dude is funny."

Funny.

That's what I wanted. To be a clown for them.

Great.

I walked away, trying not to take anything they said seriously. I went over to my backpack, turned away from everyone, and used my inhaler real fast. Then I slipped it back so nobody would see it.

Having asthma really wasn't cool.

SIX

BY THE TIME I OPENED THE DOOR TO MY HOUSE and walked up the stairs to our floor, I had already convinced myself that Kevon and Treasure would be gone. But the second I stepped into the apartment, I saw Treasure running down the hall to my room. If she was still there, I knew Kevon was, too.

I took a long, deep breath.

My mom came outta the kitchen and followed Treasure into my room. All of a sudden, it was like my room was open to *everyone*.

Two seconds later, Mom came out holding Treasure. "Jarrett," she said, "how was school?"

I shrugged.

"This little girl is a fast one," she said. "Every time I turn my back, she's off running."

I made some kinda noise, something that let her know I heard her but that I didn't really care all that much.

"You have homework?"

I shook my head even though I was supposed to read the next two chapters in this book we were reading in class. I was still tired from last night, and I didn't know if my brain could think about reading, but I had to try. I had to show Mrs. Greer I wasn't as stupid as she thought I was.

Mom went into the living room and set Treasure down. Then she reached behind the couch for this plastic cube that had a ton of toys in it. Before she even had it in her hands, Treasure was gone again, running down the hall, back to my room.

I had to see what was going on in there. So I followed her. Kevon was sitting on the bottom bunk looking miserable. Treasure ran right to him and tried to climb on his lap, but he wouldn't help her. As a matter of fact, he was trying to ignore her.

But she wasn't giving up. She tried to get on his lap again, but instead of picking her up, Kevon stood up and said, "C'mon, Treasure. Gimme a break."

That only got her to hold her arms up, but he was still ignoring her.

"She wants you to pick her up," I said, and that got Kevon's attention, because he hadn't even seen me standing there.

"I know what she wants. I'm not stupid."

"Then pick her up, genius."

"Mind your business."

Treasure started crying, still holding her arms up for Kevon. "See," I said. I mean, what did he expect her to do when her own brother wasn't paying her any attention?

All the crying still didn't get him to pick her up. He just looked down at her and said, "What's wrong with you today? I can't keep picking you up every two minutes." He moved away from her. "I gotta go to the bathroom."

He left the room, and I was stuck there with a crying baby. So I did what I always did with the foster babies: I picked her up and talked to her. I told Treasure her brother wasn't being mean, that he just had to go to the bathroom, but he was gonna play with her later. And I told her she was okay and that I could play with her if she wanted.

Most of the time, babies Treasure's age can talk. Not a lot of words, but they know how to tell you what they want. But not Treasure. Just like the caseworker said the night before, Treasure didn't talk at all. I didn't know what was wrong with her. Besides the bandage on her head, she looked fine. Normal. But maybe something was really wrong with her.

I carried Treasure back out to the living room and put her in front of the play table. Mom had taken a doll and some teacups and fake food from the cube and put it on the table already. I sat down on the floor next to the table and let Treasure give me some tea and a plate full of grapes and a hot dog. I pretended to eat and told her everything was good. And for the first time since she got there, I saw Treasure laugh, like, for real.

And me, that kinda made me feel good, too. So, even though it had been a long night and a long day, I played with Treasure for about a half hour so Mom could change Abby and cook dinner. Treasure never got tired of feeding me all that plastic food, and she laughed every time I ate something, especially when I pretended to explode from eating all that cheese and hamburgers and cake.

Mom came back into the living room after a while and gave Treasure a sippy cup with some apple juice in it, and that got Treasure to stop feeding me for a second.

"What y'all do today?" I asked Mom, but what I really meant was, "What did Kevon do today?"

"I took Kevon to the dentist. He got a couple of cavities filled, the ones that were hurting him, but he needs a lot more dental work."

Call me mean, but I was kinda happy Kevon had a worse day than me.

"Then I took Kevon and Treasure to buy them some clothes. They have very little, you know. And I had to return those shoes I bought the other day. I don't know what I was thinking, spending that kind of money on them."

My mom does that all the time. She buys something one day and takes it back to the store the next. I don't get it.

While Treasure drank her juice, I got up and tried to leave the living room, but before I could walk four steps, she ran up behind me. I turned around and saw her throw the cup down on the floor and reach her hands up. For me.

So I picked her up and tickled her. And she laughed. A lot.

The next thing I knew, Kevon was standing there. "I need to give her a bath," he said, looking at me like I was doing something wrong.

"My mom can give her a bath," I said.

"No, that's my job." He stood there waiting for me to hand her over, but I wasn't in a rush. She was having too much fun.

SEVEN

IT WAS EARLY THE NEXT MORNING, AND A BABY was crying. And that baby was in my room.

Again.

This time I couldn't hold myself back. I hung my head down from the top bunk. "You did it again, Kevon?"

"I don't know what's wrong with her."

"She's scared," I said. "She's not used to it here yet."

"Stop crying," Kevon said to Treasure. "I told you a hundred times you don't gotta cry every time you're scared."

He didn't make any sense. How else was Treasure supposed to tell him when she was scared? It wasn't her fault she couldn't talk.

I laid back down on my bed, staring up at the ceiling. I had to remind myself that it was only the second day Kevon was there. He wouldn't be here forever. I could do this.

Of course, it didn't take long for my mom to come into the room. "Kevon," she said real slow. "Didn't we talk about this yesterday?" She leaned over Kevon and picked Treasure up off the bed. Just like yesterday, the baby stopped crying right away.

"Yeah, we talked about this yesterday," Kevon said, raising his voice, "and I told you Treasure is my sister and both of us don't need nobody else."

Oh, no, I thought. *Kevon is a dead man*.

I heard my mom take a long, deep breath. "Kevon, we're not going to discuss this again. As long as you're in this house —"

"Yeah, I know," he interrupted her. "You're the boss, right?"

"Not the boss," Mom said. "This is a family, not a corporation. I'm your foster mother. I'm here to take care of you and Treasure."

"Well, what if we don't want you to take care of us? What if we're good on our own?"

I really didn't like the way he was talking to her. It was hard stopping myself from jumping in the middle of it.

"I'm not going to argue with you, Kevon. This conversation is over. If you want breakfast, get dressed and come out to the kitchen."

"I don't need your breakfast," he said. Mom left the room with Treasure and didn't pay him any mind.

Me, I couldn't ignore him the way she did. I was through with this guy. I jumped down off the top bunk. Kevon was still sitting on the bed, but I pointed my finger right in his face. "That's my mother," I said as hard and tough as I could. "And I don't like you talking to her like that. You hear me? Watch what you say to her."

"Get away from me," Kevon said. "And this is just a warning. Little boys like you shouldn't go around pointing fingers. Not unless you want them broken."

"You're threatening me?"

"You so stupid you don't know when you being threatened?"

I stared at him in the eye. "I'm not scared of you."

"Oh, yeah?" he said, getting up from the bed. And that was when I remembered how much taller he was. Still, I wasn't about to back down. We were standing there looking at each other, about an inch apart. This went on for a whole minute, the two of us staring each other down. Or *up*, in my case.

I kept my eyes on his though. I didn't look away. Finally, I said, "Stop disrespecting my mother. You wouldn't want some-one treating *your* mother like that, right?"

That got Kevon to look away from me, and I was feeling good about myself because I got him to back down. But then, after looking at the floor for a couple of seconds, he said, "I don't got a mother, alright?"

"What are you talking about?" That didn't make any sense. Didn't the caseworkers take him and Treasure away from their mother the other night?

"I'm talking about my mother," he said. "She's dead, okay?"

Dead?

His mother was dead?

It took me a while to figure out what to say to him. And when I did say something, it was stupid. "Are you sure?"

Kevon just looked at me.

I went on. "I mean, I thought when the caseworkers took you away, it was from your mom. Because that's the way it is most of the time, with the foster kids, you know?" I couldn't stop myself from running my mouth like a little kid. "So, I just thought you —"

"Stop thinking," he said. "You gonna hurt yourself."

Fine. I deserved that. "I gotta get dressed," I said, and for the first time all summer, I was actually glad I had to go to school. I had to get outta there. It was too much to deal with.

▪ ▪ ▪

After breakfast, before I left for school, my mom stopped me and told me she was gonna sign Kevon up at the Center.

"What?" I couldn't help yelling. "That's not even fair!"

"Keep your voice down."

"He's in my room," I said. "He can't hear us."

"Well, keep your voice down anyway." She looked over my shoulder like she expected Kevon to be standing there. "I'm signing him up at the Center because there's no reason that boy shouldn't be having a little fun this summer with kids his own age."

She hadn't felt that way about me when she'd signed me up for summer school.

"So make sure he knows what to do and let him meet your friends, okay?" She didn't wait for me to answer. "And walk home with him. He doesn't know this neighborhood."

"He's not from Newark?"

"Not from this side. The caseworkers didn't want to place him in a foster home too close to his own home."

"Why?"

"I'm not sure."

Of course that got my mind working overtime. There had to be a reason the caseworkers didn't want him near where he lived, and I definitely wanted to find out what it was.

"Jarrett, this is what I wanted to talk to you about," Mom continued, still whispering. "When you get to the Center, I don't want you telling everybody why Kevon is staying with us."

"*I* don't even know why Kevon is with us. Remember?"

"You know what I mean."

"But everybody already knows you're a foster mother. So why —?"

"This is different and you know it. Kevon isn't a baby. If the other kids find out he's a foster kid, they're going to ask him questions, and that might embarrass him. So if anyone asks, just tell them he's a friend of the family visiting for a few days. Those kids don't need to know all his business."

"So you're telling me to lie now?"

"Not lie. We're doing this for Kevon. He's been through a lot. There's no reason that boy needs to worry about his privacy, too."

I couldn't believe what I was hearing. Bad enough I had to deal with him in my room. Now I had to put up with him at the Center, too.

EIGHT

SUMMER SCHOOL WAS LONG AND BORING LIKE every other day. Only that day, Mrs. Greer told us we were gonna have a quiz on Friday about the book we were reading. Well, the book *they* were reading. I was just trying to follow the story by listening to everyone else talk about it in class. And sometimes Mrs. Greer read chapters out loud to us, which was better than having to read them myself.

So now I had to read a whole book in two days. I didn't think things could get worse.

Then I remembered who was gonna be at the Center.

The real truth was I didn't wanna have to face Kevon after what I'd said to him that morning. I didn't wanna have to think about his mother and her being dead and what that must even be like to not have a mom.

I mean, I didn't have a father, but neither did a lot of my friends. Mothers were different.

It was too much to think about, so I tried to put it all outta my mind.

When I got to the Center, I already knew I was late for step practice, so I ran down the hall to the room. Qasim let me in and locked the door behind me, and that was when I saw him. Kevon. He was right there in the front row like he had been part of our crew all along.

How was I supposed to put him outta my mind when he was right there?

Me and Kevon looked at each other for half a second. Then I just took my place in the second row behind all the taller guys who actually knew what they were doing.

Step class is hard enough when you're trying to memorize all the moves and get your feet and arms to do what they're supposed to do. But when your mind isn't on it, it's practically impossible.

"Man, your cousin is good," Hector said when we were taking a break. "We need a guy like that on our crew."

It took me about five seconds to figure out what he was talking about. He was calling Kevon my cousin? When did *friend of the family* turn into *cousin*?

None of this was okay with me.

We definitely didn't need Kevon on our crew. Why would we? Just to make the rest of us look bad?

Anyway, Kevon wasn't even gonna be with us by the time the block party came around. That wasn't till Labor Day at the beginning of September, almost a whole month away. I figured there wasn't anything to worry about.

After practice, the other guys hung around talking to Kevon. They were all laughing about some joke they'd played that morning on Miss Lisa, the cafeteria lady, and Kevon was acting like he'd known those guys his whole life.

I couldn't take it anymore. I tried to leave the room real fast, but Kevon caught up to me in the hall and said, "That was hard." Like I believed that.

Anyway, I was only half listening to him. It was hard to think of anything when Caprice was walking down the hall with her friends. And it was hard not to stare at her like some kinda hungry dog. But no matter how hard I tried to move my eyes off of her, I couldn't do it.

She was so pretty. Not in the same way as her best friend, Nicole. Everybody could see Nicole was pretty because she made sure of it. She always had on something pink or glittery or sparkly. And since her last name was Valentine, she made sure there were hearts on her backpack and notebooks and pens and stuff. Everything. All the time.

But Caprice was different, and that's what I liked about her. She didn't do all that fancy stuff. Her hair was in locs that she always put up in a ponytail. Sometimes I wished she would leave it out so I could see how long it was, but Caprice wasn't the type to care about that. At least, I didn't think she was. Anyway, she didn't need to try that hard to look cute.

That day she had on white shorts that I never saw before and a red belt that looked kinda like a rope. And she had on a black tank top with *Georgia Peach* written on it. And she was wearing mismatched Converse sneakers, one red and one white.

Cute.

It didn't hurt that she was shorter than me. That's another thing I liked about her, especially since most of the girls were already my height or taller.

As the group of girls walked past me, Caprice smiled and wiggled her fingers with black-and-white-striped nail polish at me. "Hi, Jarrett," she said, but she didn't wait for me to say anything back. She just kept on walking down the hall.

I stood there with my mouth open, like I wanted to say something, but then I couldn't do anything to close it. It was like the hinge was broken or something. But that's the way it's been for a while. I used to be able to talk to Caprice like she was a regular person, but a few months ago that changed and now I couldn't even figure out how to say hi to her anymore.

"What are we supposed to be doing now, Jared?" Kevon asked me.

"My name is Jarrett," I said, hardly paying any attention to him.

"Are we supposed to be somewhere, *Jarrett*?"

"Huh?" If Ennis had been there, we probably would have gone into the art room to work on new ideas for our masks. But he still wasn't back.

I really didn't want Kevon hanging around with me all day. Why couldn't he look up at the board and figure out what he wanted to do on his own? The other kids were calling him my cousin, but he was starting to feel like my Siamese twin.

"*I'm* going to the gym," I told him.

"Cool," he said. "It's been a while since I shot some hoops."

I turned to walk down the hall. Even before we got to the gym, I knew what was gonna happen. Kevon was gonna be just as good at basketball as he was at step. And he was gonna make me look like even more of a loser than I already was.

NINE

I WISH I COULD SAY THE NEXT DAY WAS BETTER, but it wasn't. It was Thursday and Kevon had been invading my territory for two and a half days. I was trying not to stress out about it, but inside I was getting worried. What if it took a long time for the caseworkers to find a new home for Kevon and Treasure? Ennis was coming back from Jamaica on Friday, and me and him had plans for Saturday, plans that would be all messed up if Kevon was still there.

After I got home from the Center and ate dinner, I spent a couple minutes playing with Treasure, then I went to my room to try to read the book for the test. The book was 192 pages, and I knew I couldn't read the whole thing anymore. No way was that gonna happen.

But I came up with a plan. I was gonna read the first page and the last page of every chapter, and I would try to figure out what happened in between. It was better than not reading anything.

I sat at my desk and opened the book. I knew what the story was about from the parts Mrs. Greer read to us. It was about some boy who was in a plane crash and got lost out in the middle of, like, these woods all by himself. He had to figure out how to survive.

I wished this book was a movie because it might be kinda cool. I could see myself making the trailer for it. It would be real exciting with lots of action and fast camera shots, and the boy running away from bears and coyotes and stuff. I would put in a lot of real loud sound effects, too.

Most people don't know this, but the trailer is the most important thing in Hollywood. The trailer is how you get people to even wanna come and see a movie. My video teacher, Lawrence, said, "A good trailer will put butts in the movie theater seats." I could make a trailer for this book that would put a butt in every seat in every theater in the whole country.

But reading the book was another thing.

Not only couldn't I get my brain to concentrate on the words on the page, every time I was able to read a couple of paragraphs, Treasure would run into my room and climb up on my lap. Then Kevon would come in to get her so he could give her her bath. This happened twice before I closed the door. My mother wouldn't let me put a lock on it, but the handle is too high for babies to reach.

But that didn't stop Kevon from coming in by himself, first to get something outta his army bag, then to put it back. And of course while he was in there, Treasure came running through the door he left open. The whole situation was driving me insane.

Finally, I couldn't take it anymore. "Can you stop coming in here?" I asked Kevon after Treasure ran outta the room again. I tried to keep my voice calm . . . which was hard.

"What's your problem?" he asked.

"You came in here about a thousand times already!"

"Calm down. You're acting like a child."

"Because you're *so* much older, right?" This guy was getting to me.

"When I was eleven I wasn't a baby like you," he said. "Look how you act."

"Look how you smell," I said.

He busted out laughing. "You so stupid."

I couldn't think of anything else to say, so I just went with, "Get outta my room, stupid."

He stared at me for a long time, trying to intimidate me. Then he smiled and said, "Whatever you say, stupid." But he didn't move.

"I'm serious, stupid."

He shook his head. "You're a waste of time, stupid."

"I said get outta my room, stupid. How stupid are you, stupid?"

"I'm not the stupid one in summer school, am I?" He left the room before I could think of anything to say back to him. I stood there for a long time, staring at the door, trying to come up with something so I could go out there and tell him off.

But my mom was out there, and if I said anything to him, I would have to deal with her. So I tried to calm myself down. When I was little, I always wanted my mother to have another baby so I could have a brother, but I must have been crazy or something. Why would I want someone like that around all the time?

I didn't have any time to think about that. I would have to deal with him later, when it was just me and him. That night, I had work to do. I had to find a way to get outta sixth grade.

I opened the book again, but I would be lying if I said I wasn't still thinking about Kevon and what he said. I stared at the words and tried to see the story in my mind, but it was hard. Maybe I was too mad to understand what I was reading.

Or maybe Kevon was right about me.

▪ ▪ ▪

"Jared? Jared?" Kevon's voice woke me up. I hadn't said a word to him the whole rest of the night, and even in my sleep, he was still bothering me. "You awake?"

"*Now* I am." I sat up, mad. What was this guy waking me up in the middle of the night for? "And my name is Jarrett, not Jared. How many times do I have to tell you that?"

"Whatever," he said. "I'm just letting you know that your mother's man is fighting with her. You gonna let that happen?"

If he didn't say anything, I probably wouldn't have heard my mom and Terrence. But now that he said something, I could hear them in one of the other rooms. "They're not fighting," I said. "They're just talking."

At least that's what my mom always told me. She said it was nothing, that her and Terrence just talked louder than normal sometimes.

That night, I didn't know what Kevon was so worried about. They weren't even as loud as they got sometimes. They definitely weren't screaming at each other or anything. All I heard were little bits of sentences.

". . . gonna take time off," Terrence said.

My mom said something back, but I couldn't hear it.

Then Terrence said something like, "We need to make time."

"I can't," my mom said. "I have a full house."

Then they went on and on, and it was just the same thing over and over. Terrence was always trying to get my mom to take a break from taking new babies so they could go away somewhere and have a vacation or something. But my mom acted like there weren't any other foster mothers in Newark, or at least none as good as her.

"Just go to sleep," I told Kevon. "It's nothing. They're gonna make up in, like, five minutes. Watch."

"Alright. I was just trying to look out for your mom."

I almost said, "Thanks," but I didn't. He acted like he needed to protect my mom when he didn't have to. If she needed protection, that was what *I* was there for.

TEN

I KNEW I WAS DOOMED, EVEN FROM THE FIRST question. First of all, it wasn't multiple choice. I might have had a chance if all I had to do was pick the right answer. But Mrs. Greer wasn't nice like that. She was out to get us.

Especially me.

The test was the kind where she asked a question and we had to write the answer on a bunch of lines. I read all of the questions, and it was no use even trying. I didn't know anything.

Even if I had read the book, I probably wouldn't have remembered any of it anyway. Not with everything going on in my house.

"Have a good weekend, everyone," Mrs. Greer said as we were leaving.

Most of the boys said good-bye to her, but not me. She didn't want me to have a good weekend. She wanted me to fail so everyone would know she was right about me.

I left without saying anything and walked down the hall mad. Everything was a mess.

▪ ▪ ▪

When I got to the Center, I looked up at the board and all it said was *Trip to Tennis Center.* Everybody — even Kevon — was gone, which wasn't even fair. There wasn't anything else to do, so I found my friend Yu in the parking lot outside, and he tried to teach me some skateboard tricks for a while. I fell so many times, it didn't even hurt anymore. It was like my body went numb or something. It was fun though.

I got home late with my knee all busted up.

"Mom, I'm bleeding!" I practically screamed as I came through the door.

"There are Band-Aids in the bathroom." She was straightening up the living room, with Abby in the baby holder strapped to the front of her body. Treasure was playing on the floor with Rafa, this kid from down the street that my mom babysits for sometimes. They were playing with a whole bunch of plastic cups, stacking them up and knocking them down with a fire truck and an old Hess truck that used to be mine. They were so into what they were doing, I don't even think they saw me there.

"Where?" I asked.

"Look in the cabinet over the sink."

I stood there for a couple of seconds because most of the time she would get the Band-Aids for me. But it looked like she was too busy with all her other kids to help her real one.

So I went down the hall. In the bathroom, I grabbed a Band-Aid and sat on the side of the bathtub to survey the damage to my knee. It was nasty and covered with dirt and blood. At the same time, it was kinda cool, the way it looked. I thought about creating a mask with cuts like this all over the face with blood oozing out. I couldn't wait to give Ennis that idea.

I cleaned up the cut the best way I could and put the Band-Aid on it. Then I heard Kevon's voice coming from the living room. He was back already, telling my mom all about the trip. "It was really cool," he said. "I never played tennis before."

"Never?" Mom asked. "Well, there's a first time for everything, right?"

I never played tennis either. Probably never would now.

"I wanna go back," Kevon told my mom. Then he started telling her about every single thing he did and how much fun he had.

The way Mom was talking to him, you would think it was more important than seeing if my knee was infected or anything.

But maybe that was a good thing. She was so busy she would probably forget to ask me how I did on that stupid test. I hated to admit it, but Kevon was good for something.

Back in the living room, Mom was still cleaning up. "The caseworker is on her way," she said, and me and Kevon looked at each other real fast. The caseworker was coming to get him. He was going back home today.

Finally.

I started to smile, but I stopped when I saw the look on Kevon's face. He didn't look as happy as I thought he would be.

"My f-father," he started, and it was hard to read his face. He kinda looked scared to me, but why would he look like that? "They found him?"

"*Found* him?" I asked, and that was when my mom shot me

one of those looks, the kind that was supposed to remind me to be *sensitive* and not get in Kevon's business. But I couldn't help it. I needed to know what was going on with Kevon's father.

"I'll go pack," Kevon said, and he started walking down the hall.

"No, Kevon," Mom said, and he stopped. "Sweetheart, this isn't your caseworker. It's Abby's caseworker who's coming. Abby's aunt is going to take her until her mom gets out of rehab and gets her life together."

I should have known my luck wasn't that good. I wasn't gonna get rid of Kevon that fast.

"What about me?" Kevon asked. "They didn't — ?"

"No, you and Treasure are going to be staying with us this weekend. Your caseworker couldn't find a new home for you. She's still looking. Either way, she'll be here Monday to see you and Treasure."

Kevon looked down at the floor and let out a long breath.

Me, my whole body slumped. Kevon was gonna be here all weekend. My plans with Ennis were gonna be ruined.

■ ■ ■

The caseworker got there about fifteen minutes later, after Mom finished cleaning up. Mom got Abby ready and took a picture with her the way she always does when the babies are leaving, and that was it. Abby was gone.

My mom got sad for a little while, as usual. But not me. Babies have been coming and going in my house since I could remember. When I was little I used to get attached to them, thinking they were my new little brother or sister or something. Then they would be gone, and I would cry and be all mad. It took me a while to stop being that dumb and figure out that all of them were gonna leave and I couldn't do anything about it.

The thing is, after Abby left, I kept thinking about what my mom said when the caseworker asked her if she was available for another foster baby. She said yes, without even thinking about it. Just like that.

My mom went into the kitchen to wash dishes. "Keep an eye on the kids for me," she said to me. "Rafa keeps trying to rip Treasure's bandage off." Kevon could have watched them, but he was in my room with the door closed.

"I thought you were gonna stop taking babies for a little while," I said, keeping my voice down. "I mean, didn't Terrence say —"

"That's not your concern, Jarrett," she said. "What happens between Terrence and me is grown-folks' business."

I shook my head. If they wanted it to stay grown-folks' business, they shouldn't be arguing all loud in the middle of the night. That's what I wanted to say to her, but of course, I didn't. My mother wasn't the kind to put up with that. I knew that from experience. A lot of it.

So I just went back into the living room without saying anything, sat on the floor with Treasure and Rafa, who were laughing and having more fun than I was having that day. I stacked up the cups for them, just so they could keep knocking them down.

Something about that made sense to me.

ELEVEN

I JUMPED OUTTA BED THE NEXT MORNING. IT WAS like I didn't know how much I wanted Ennis back till right then. Three weeks is a long time to be away, especially in the middle of the summer, and the middle of our production schedule.

Kevon was still sleeping, so I left the room real quiet. In the kitchen, Mom and Terrence were at the table having coffee. Mom was holding Treasure on her lap, trying to get her to eat some oatmeal, but as soon as she saw me, she squirmed her way outta my mom's arms and ran over to me. I picked her up, and she giggled.

I wished she could talk. I wanted to know if she knew my name already. "You think she's ever gonna know how to talk?" I asked my mom.

"She was supposed to be getting speech therapy and occupational therapy, but she hasn't gone for months."

"Why not?" I knew I was getting into one of those areas that Mom would say was confidential. But that didn't mean I didn't wanna know.

"There was a lot going on in the family," she said. "It's complicated. And private."

I was never gonna get answers outta her.

Treasure kissed me on the cheek, one of those wet, messy baby kisses. I held her up real high — well, as high as a guy my size could get — then brought her down real low, and she laughed just like I knew she was gonna.

Finally, my mom said, "Okay, Jarrett. You're making that girl dizzy."

I set Treasure down on the floor, but of course she wanted me to pick her up again, which I did. I just didn't swing her around anymore.

She was one of the foster kids I could get used to having around. Too bad she had to leave when Kevon did.

"When is she gonna get this thing off?" I asked my mom, rubbing Treasure's bandage.

"The stitches come out next week. I just hope she doesn't have a scar."

I never thought about that. I wouldn't want her to have a big scar on her forehead either.

"I have to go back to Macy's to return a dress," Mom said. "And I'll stop by the supermarket on my way back. So make a list of what you boys want to eat at your slumber party."

I hated when she said *slumber party*. It made me and Ennis sound like we were nine-year-old girls who were gonna stay awake and polish each other's toenails, instead of two guys who were working on a major film project.

"Can we make tacos?" I asked. "We never have them."

"Write down everything you need, all the ingredients."

She didn't need me to tell her what to buy for tacos, but I knew what she was doing. She was trying to get me to write, like that was gonna help me pass the sixth-grade test next week. So I sat down and wrote out the list anyway even though Treasure kept trying to grab the pen outta my hand the whole time.

■ ■ ■

Aunt Inez came over around 2:00. On Saturday night Mom and Terrence always took off on a date, and they didn't get home until real late, so Aunt Inez stayed over. Sometimes Mom stayed over at Terrence's house and came home in the morning. All of that was fine with me because Ennis always spent the night with me. We hung out in the living room where the TV was, and Aunt Inez took care of the babies while Mom was out having fun.

Aunt Inez isn't really my aunt. She's kinda my mom's aunt, but not really. When my mom was, like, around my age, she moved from Guyana to New Jersey by herself so she could go to a better school and then go to college. Aunt Inez let her live with her, and she took care of her. Then, when I was born, Aunt Inez helped my mom take care of me, too, because Mom was only twenty-one years old and didn't really know anything about babies. Now, all she does is take care of them.

When Mom got back from the store, I inspected the bags. Taco stuff, check. Junk food, check. Ice cream, check. "Where's the soda?"

"No soda," Mom said. "There's enough sugar in the cookies and ice cream. I'm going to make you boys some Crystal Light."

"Oh, my God!"

"Or would you prefer water?"

I shook my head and mumbled, "Crystal Light."

She smiled.

Aunt Inez started in on Mom in her thick Guyanese accent. "You spoil the little boy, buying him all this foolishness. Cook the boy some real food, Kimma."

"It's the weekend, Inez. He's been eating real food all week. Anyway, I need to leave soon."

"You need to spend more time with him," Aunt Inez said. "I keep telling you that."

"I know," Mom said. "And I do."

Aunt Inez sucked her teeth.

"Where's Kevon?" Mom asked me. I knew she was changing the subject, and I didn't blame her.

"In my room with Treasure."

"I hope you and Ennis won't forget about him tonight. You need to include him in your sleepover."

"But that's not even fair!"

"You can't be rude to your company. There's no reason why he can't watch the movie with you boys."

"But we're gonna be working on our movie trailer, too."

"Then get him to help. He can paint the masks or help you —"

"We're still writing the trailer!"

"Give him a chance, Jarrett. He might have some good ideas, too."

This was so messed up. Just because *she* wanted to bring kids into the house, why did that mean I had to get stuck hanging out with them?

Terrence came outta the bedroom, and I asked him if me and Ennis could use his laptop to work on our movie trailer that night. He said okay, that he would get it for me when he went home to feed and walk his dogs.

One time, I heard Terrence ask my mom to move into his house with him, that his place was big enough for everyone and that I would even get to play in his backyard. But my mom said no. She said she didn't want the babies around his dogs, that it wasn't safe for them.

The babies again. Everything she did was about the babies.

TWELVE

THAT NIGHT, MOM AND TERRENCE GOT ALL DRESSED up for their date. Mom looked real good in a red dress and shoes with really high heels. Even though she spent a lot of time with Treasure, every time she headed for the front door, Treasure wanted to be picked up again, till Terrence had to put his arm around Mom's waist and tell her they had to leave if they didn't wanna be late for the show.

A second after they left, Treasure lost her mind crying. Aunt Inez picked her up, but that didn't work. "I'm going to take this one out for a walk," she said to me. "You boys behave yourself here."

"Of course," I said. Kevon was in my room, acting weird, so it wasn't like me and him were gonna do anything stupid together.

When Aunt Inez left with Treasure, I started setting up the sleeping bags in the living room. I put the Cheetos and cookies in bowls, and since Mom had already made all the stuff that went into the tacos, all I had to do was wait for Ennis to get there.

Every summer I had to go through this, Ennis going away and me being left by myself. I mean, the other guys at the

Center were alright, but they weren't Ennis. Me and him started to be friends when we were two or three or something, after my mom started watching him whenever his mother had to work a double shift at the hospital.

This time, Ennis hardly stepped into the apartment before I attacked him. I grabbed him fast and pulled him into the living room and down to the floor. That was my tactic, to surprise him, catch him off guard. I was just about to celebrate when a second later, he flipped me over and pinned me. "Don't forget who's stronger," he said.

"Get off!" I tried to get out from under him, but he had me.

"Say the words."

"Okay," I said. "You win. You win." I was never gonna get him, and I'd been trying for years. He was just much bigger — not fat or anything, but solid. A guy my size was never gonna be a match for him.

Ennis let me go, and then me and him started laughing, right there on the floor, like we were little kids or something. I wasn't gonna let him know, but I was real happy he was back.

After Ennis told me about all the cool stuff he got to do in Jamaica, he jumped up and said, "We got a lot of work to do. Like *a lot*."

"I know. I have some good ideas."

"You wrote them down?"

"No, I got them all right here." I tapped my head.

"You gotta write them down," he said. "Let's get started so we have time to watch the movie."

He headed down the hall, like he was going to my room to get the masks and stuff. "We can't go in there," I said, getting up off the floor. "I got . . . My mom got . . . Somebody's in there."

He stopped. "Who?"

"Kevon." I knew I had to explain the whole situation to him, so I made him come back in the living room to tell him who Kevon was and all that.

"He can help with the movie, then," Ennis said after I told him everything.

"No, we don't need him."

Ennis shook his head, but he didn't understand everything. He wasn't the one stuck with some stranger sleeping in his room.

Since Kevon was still in my room doing whatever he was doing, me and Ennis set up everything in the living room: Terrence's laptop, our storyboards, and of course the junk food.

Me and Ennis made a good team. We came up with the story together, but he did most of the writing. He was a good artist, too, so he was the one who designed all the masks even though we both made them. I was in charge of shooting the whole trailer and doing all the editing, because I was the one learning how to become a filmmaker at the Center.

While Ennis opened Terrence's laptop and got started on the script, I grabbed the big sketchbook outta his backpack and flipped through it. He practically filled the whole thing while he was in Jamaica. When I got to the end, I saw that he had another one in his backpack, a little one. I reached over to grab it, but he said, "No, there's nothing in that one. I just got it."

"Then let's work," I said.

I had so many ideas for the trailer, and I couldn't wait to tell him. A few minutes later the ideas were coming in real fast. "And the monsters come out from behind the Dumpsters!" I said. "And —"

"And they creep up to the victim!" Ennis said as he kept typing.

This story was practically writing itself. "And then it's gonna start raining and —"

"Hey, how are we gonna make it rain, Jarrett? We don't have that kind of budget."

"But it would be cool if every time the monsters came out it started raining."

"Yeah, but we can't do it."

I didn't like when Ennis got practical. "Yes, we can. Lawrence can help us figure it out. See, the monsters live behind the Dumpsters, right? And when they come out, it always starts raining outta nowhere, and when it rains, everybody knows something bad is gonna happen."

Ennis nodded. "And we can put in some creepy music."

"Yeah!" I said. "That's gonna be crazy scary. All the girls are gonna freak out and they're gonna hold hands with any boy that's sitting next to them. I know who *I'm* gonna sit with." I couldn't help but start smiling. It was gonna work out perfect.

Ennis pushed the laptop over to me. "Okay, you write some now."

"Why? You write way better than me."

"You have to try, Jarrett. How are you gonna get better if you don't try?"

"It's gonna take me too long." Why was he making this so hard?

"No it's not. Just type everything we say. It's easy."

"Easy for you," I said, "because you're smart."

"You're smart, too."

I just shook my head. I didn't wanna tell him about Mrs. Greer and what I heard her say about me.

Ennis started looking mad at me or something. "C'mon, Jarrett. If you don't work on your writing and reading, how are you gonna pass summer school? What are you gonna do, just fail and make me have to do seventh grade by myself?"

Me and him stared at each other for a couple of seconds. Summer school didn't have anything to do with him. Why was he making everything about him when *I* was the one who would be stuck in sixth grade, not him? He was going to seventh grade no matter what.

"Alright," I said. "I'll write, but only for a little while."

Me and Ennis worked on the movie for about another half hour, till I started to get tired from writing. "Let's work on the masks," I said, closing the laptop.

Then I remembered, the masks and all the art stuff were in the trunk in my room, and I had to go in there and deal with Kevon just to get it.

"You sure you don't wanna ask him if he wants to help us?" Ennis asked. "What's he doing anyway?"

I shrugged. "Being bored probably."

"I feel bad for him. Ask him if he wants to work with us and watch the movie."

"I don't know. He's probably not into this kinda stuff."

"Just go see."

I went down the hall to my room. Kevon was sitting on the floor looking through one of my horror magazines. And his big army bag was on top of my trunk.

"What are you doing?" I asked him.

"Nothing."

"I need to get in the trunk."

"Your friend still here?" he asked, getting up.

"Yeah, he's spending the night. Me and him are gonna work on the masks and watch a movie. Do you — I mean, if you're not doing anything, you can help us."

He shrugged and picked his bag up off the trunk so I could open it.

"And we have tacos. If you're hungry."

"I never had tacos before."

"That's weird." I grabbed the masks and the paint kit. "Here. Can you take these while I grab the heads?"

"Heads?"

I pulled out one of the white styrofoam heads.

"That's freaky," Kevon said.

"They're really for wigs," I told him, "but we use them when we're painting the masks."

I only had two heads, so I grabbed them and the blue tarp, and me and him walked back out to the living room. I laid out the tarp so we didn't get any paint on the rug.

"Ennis, this is Kevon, my, um . . ." I didn't even know what to call him.

"What's up?" Kevon said to Ennis.

"What's up?" Ennis said back.

Then that was it. Nobody had anything else to say.

It was getting awkward. "Let's make some tacos," I said. At least it would be something we could do. So we didn't have to talk.

All three of us went to the kitchen, and I started showing Kevon how to put the tacos together. "I can't believe you never had a taco before," I said. I wasn't sure where he came from, but wherever it was, he never got out much.

We put our tacos on plates and brought everything into the living room so we could eat, paint the masks, and watch the movie, all at the same time. Ennis had the remote control, and he started scrolling through the movies till he found *Circus of Terror*. Before I even had taken two bites, even before the opening credits, the first head was cut off and went rolling down the street. I don't know why, but we all started laughing.

That was when Aunt Inez came home with Treasure, who ran through the living room, across the tarp, and right into my lap. My taco flew outta my hand, and everything — the shell and all the fillings — landed on the tarp next to me.

"Treasure!" I tried to keep my voice down, but I couldn't. "You can't do that."

Behind me, Aunt Inez sucked her teeth. "Your mother, I don't know why she lets you kids eat in the living room."

"We're on the tarp, Aunt Inez," I answered.

She shook her head.

I would never win that fight. "Pause the movie," I said to Ennis. "I gotta clean this up." I got up and tried to pick up as much stuff as I could from off the tarp, but it was a mess. Treasure tried to help me, which was nice considering it was her fault, but almost-two-year-olds aren't any good at cleaning up. They mostly just make a bigger mess, which is what Treasure did.

When the tarp was cleaned off and Aunt Inez took Treasure into my mom's room, we finally had the living room to ourselves again. We went back to the movie, and when we were finished eating, we got the wig heads set up and started working on the masks. Kevon wasn't an artist like Ennis, but he was okay.

No better or worse than me.

THIRTEEN

AT THE CENTER ON MONDAY, I WAS KINDA HOPING I would get up the nerve to talk to Caprice. Just talk, like, say some actual words to her. If I couldn't even talk to her, how was I ever gonna be able to tell her how I was feeling about her?

Ennis was in the art room by himself, sitting at one of the tables. His back was to me, but I could tell by the way he was sitting that he was drawing something, probably in that little sketchbook he had at my house on Saturday.

I came into the room and walked over to the table. "Here you are," I said.

Real fast, Ennis closed the sketchbook. "What's up, Jarrett?" he asked, trying to look like I wasn't interrupting him, but I knew I was. And the weird thing was, he wasn't actually sketching in that book. He was writing.

Was Ennis keeping a diary or something?

"We're gonna have step practice now," I told him. "You should join our crew."

"Crew?"

"Yeah, crew." I explained to him about what we were doing, and how we were trying to surprise everybody, especially the girls, at the block party.

"I told Mrs. Prajapati I was gonna teach some of the little kids how to draw," he said. "She wants them to have some artwork to show everyone at the block party."

"Oh." It was weird. I wasn't used to doing different things from Ennis. But if he didn't wanna do step, what was I supposed to do? "Alright. I'll catch up to you then."

I walked back outta the room, kinda waiting for him to change his mind. When I turned around, he had his head down again and was back to writing in that little book.

▪ ▪ ▪

I didn't see Caprice before step practice, but afterward, as soon as me and Kevon walked outta the room, there she was, walking down the hall with Nicole and some other girls. They were all wearing different color tank tops and these weird black pants that were kinda tight.

I don't understand girls. Why did they always have to walk around with so many other girls? How were boys supposed to talk to them when they were always in a pack?

I was just staring at Caprice, not saying anything. Good thing she said something to me first. Again.

"Hey, Jarrett," she said, smiling.

So cute.

"Um, hi," I said back. Two words. Well, one of them

might not even be a word, but it was better than nothing, like last time.

All the girls kept walking down the hall and went into one of the classrooms. I looked up at the big board, trying to figure out what they were up to. That's when I saw what was going on in there. *Room 108: Introduction to Yoga*.

"I'm gonna go play basketball," Kevon said. But I wasn't listening. I was already walking toward Room 108.

"Where you going?" Kevon called after me.

"Where do you think?"

"You serious?" he asked.

I didn't have time to talk. "Look, Kevon. You coming or what?"

I didn't wanna be late for yoga.

■ ■ ■

Yoga isn't easy. That was the first thing I found out that day. I was only, like, two minutes into the class, standing on my mat trying to touch the floor, but only the tips of my fingers could touch without bending my legs.

With my head hanging down like that, I had to admit, my feet smelled kinda like hot cheese. About five minutes later, that's the way the whole room smelled. All the girls turned around to look at me and Kevon, like only boys have stink feet.

It wouldn't have been so bad if Kevon wasn't looking at me with the same expression on his face that the girls had. Next thing I knew, everyone knew whose feet it was.

And it wasn't only the smell. When I gave my feet a good look, they were bad. Real bad. My toenails were all long and dirty, and my feet were dry and ashy. My mom was always telling me to cut my toenails, but who had time to do that? Anyway, it wasn't like I *planned* to take a yoga class or anything.

I kinda wanted to run outta there, but I didn't. Because the best thing about yoga class was, it was full of girls! If it wasn't for me and Kevon, it would have been *all* girls. So I stayed, and so did Kevon.

Touching my toes was easy compared to everything else they wanted me to do. There's some crazy moves in yoga, moves they call "poses" that got crazy animal names, stuff like *dolphin, downward dog, happy puppy, camel*, and *cobra*. You never really look like the animal you're supposed to be though.

I don't think people's bodies are supposed to get into so many twisted animal poses. Definitely not boys' bodies.

It hurt.

Another thing, if you make your body go in those positions, especially that extended puppy pose, you're gonna have to rip one. Or two. Or five. Not my fault. But if the smell of hot-cheese feet was bad, the smell of hot cheese *and* gas was deadly. The teacher practically ran and opened the door as soon as class was over.

I pushed my feet back into my sneakers real fast, like that was gonna take the smell outta the room. Didn't work. It would take days or months for that room to air out.

Kids started leaving the room, and I thought about going up to Caprice to tell her she was good at yoga. But at the same time, I didn't want her to know I'd been staring at her practically the whole time.

She came up to me instead, and she didn't say anything about my feet. "I didn't know you were into yoga, Jarrett," she said.

"Yeah, I'm not like all those other guys," I said, then thought, *That was a full sentence*. I started to feel more confident, so I kept talking. "Most guys think it's a waste of time to get in touch with their, um, you know, spiritual side." Even as the words came outta my mouth, I knew it was a slam dunk. Or a three-pointer.

That's because Caprice smiled so big and said, "I know! Everybody needs to take time to take care of themselves."

I nodded. "I feel the same way."

I think me and her were about to have a real connection, but then Kevon messed it up. He came up to me, right in front of Caprice, like she wasn't even there, and said, "Remember, I have to get back to your place early today."

I tried to ignore him and just look at Caprice instead, but he wouldn't go away. "C'mon, Jared."

That did it. "Jarrett," I said slow, looking at him with the maddest face I could make. "It's Jarrett."

Caprice laughed. "I thought you were cousins."

I shook my head. "Not real cousins." I could feel Kevon's eyes burning into my neck. "His mom and my mom are, like, best friends. Something like that."

I didn't even know what lie I was supposed to be telling anymore. And I know I shouldn't have said anything about his mom, but it was the first thing I could think to say. It was getting all confusing.

"You gonna go back with me?" Kevon asked.

I knew Kevon and Treasure's caseworker was coming by to see them, and I couldn't miss that. So I told Caprice I'd see her the next day and, hard as it was, I left with Kevon. I had to study anyway.

There would be more time for Caprice after summer school was over. I just needed to keep reminding myself of that.

FOURTEEN

WHEN WE GOT HOME, THE CASEWORKER WASN'T there yet. "Good," Mom said when we came through the door. "You're early." She was in the kitchen scooping coffee outta the canister and putting it into the coffeemaker.

"Did we have a choice?" I mumbled. Mom turned around and shot me one of those looks, so I figured it was best to change the subject, fast. "We took yoga," I said.

"Yoga?" Mom turned back to the coffeemaker. "At the Center?"

"Yeah. They're gonna have it every Monday."

"They need to have a class like that for adults. I could use it to unwind after a day like today."

I took a step into the kitchen, and Mom sniffed me and said, "Did you put on deodorant this morning, Jarrett?"

"I, um, yeah."

"No, you didn't." Her face was all screwed up like I was the stinkiest thing on the planet. "Do I really have to tell you the same thing every day?"

I took a step back so my funkiness wouldn't kill her. I looked in the living room where Treasure was rolling around on the floor with Rafa. Kevon was standing over them, watching. Not playing with them. Just watching. "What happened today?" I asked my mom.

"Treasure had a rough day. A lot of crying. She's probably homesick."

"She looks okay now."

"Yeah, she took a long nap, and when she woke up, she was feeling better. Poor little baby."

I wondered who she was homesick for. I didn't know anything about their life before they came here. All I knew was their mother was dead. I needed to know more.

I told Mom I had to study for my test, and I went into my room and closed the door. I sat at my desk and even studied for a little while, just in case she came in to check on me. But I was just waiting till the caseworker got there.

It took about twenty minutes, and after I gave everyone time to settle down and for Mom to serve her coffee, I opened my bedroom door and peeked out. By the sound of it, everyone was in the living room. I wanted to listen in, but now wasn't the time. I needed to wait till Mom left the living room so that the caseworker could talk to Kevon by himself. That was when I'd find out everything I needed to know.

Sure enough, Mom came outta the living room with Treasure and Rafa, and she took them into the kitchen with her. This was my opportunity.

I crept down the hall silently, since I had a whole lot of practice doing it. Then I slowly opened the door to the hall closet and ducked inside, leaving it open just a crack. It wasn't perfect, but when there wasn't too much noise coming from Mom and the babies, I could hear Kevon and the caseworker talking in the living room.

"I want to go over this with you again," the caseworker said, "because we're having a lot of trouble locating your father."

"I *told* you," Kevon said, almost sounding mad. "He went to Detroit for a job, a construction job for three weeks."

"Did he tell you the name of the company he was working for, or where he was going to be staying?"

"No," Kevon said. "He just said they were gonna pay him more than he was making in Newark, and we needed the money."

"When was the last time you spoke with him?"

"About two days before, you know, before Treasure got hurt."

"And did your father call you or did you call him?"

"He doesn't have a phone where he's at. He called us whenever he found a phone he could use."

"And what is the name of the woman he hired to babysit you and Treasure?"

"I already told you," Kevon said. "Her name is Diana. I don't know her last name."

"The last time we talked, you told me her name was Donna."

"No, not Donna. Diana."

"And what happened to Donna/Diana?"

"I don't know," Kevon said. "When Treasure fell and hurt herself, Diana took off before the ambulance got there. I think she was afraid everyone was going to blame her, when it wasn't anyone's fault. It was an accident."

"Did you know Diana for a long time?"

"Yeah, kinda. She babysits us sometimes when my father has to work late. But I don't know where she lives, if that's what you wanna know."

"Kevon, in the past, I know your dad has had some problems. Has he been taking his medication? Is that what —?"

"He's not crazy!" Kevon said, his voice a lot louder than before. "He's a good father."

"Okay, okay. It's just that something about this whole thing doesn't make sense. Your father hasn't been able to reach you kids for a week now. Why hasn't he come home? We've left so many letters under your apartment door letting him know he has to call us, but so far, nothing."

"The job was supposed to last, um, four weeks," Kevon said. "When it's over, he's gonna come home and take us back."

Standing in that closet, listening to this, I knew Kevon was lying. He couldn't even keep his facts straight. The caseworker probably knew he was lying, too, because she said, "Are you sure your father wasn't home when Treasure got hurt, Kevon? We need to know the truth about what happened."

"He wasn't there," Kevon said. "We were there with Donna."

"Don't you mean Diana?" the caseworker asked.

"Yeah, I mean Diana. You're getting me all confused."

Kevon wasn't confused at all. He was making that story up as he went along. He was definitely hiding something — and I wanted to know what it was.

FIFTEEN

AFTER SCHOOL THE NEXT DAY, I DIDN'T EVEN GET all the way to the Center when I saw a cop car parked in front. Nothing new about that around my neighborhood, but still, I wanted to know what was going on. Who did what.

As I got closer though, I started to see who it was.

Qasim.

I wanted to see and hear everything, but for some reason, my legs started walking slower. I wasn't scared or anything, but I kinda didn't wanna see what was happening. Because it was bad.

There was two police officers and I saw one of them put his hands on Qasim's back and push him up against the police car hard. Then the other cop frisked him, patting him down like he thought he was carrying a gun or something illegal.

I mean, who would think Qasim would do something like that? Qasim started to say something, but one of the cops told him to stop talking. I couldn't really believe what I was seeing, or that this was happening right here where people were walking on the sidewalk and kids were running in and outta the Center.

It didn't make any sense.

I walked a little closer but tried not to let the cops see me and throw me against a car, too. I wanted to stop them. Help Qasim. But what could I do?

The cop was still searching Qasim, putting his hands all over his legs, up and down one leg and then the other. Qasim looked like he wanted to get away, but the other cop kinda held him on the car. "What are y'all looking for?" Qasim asked, real mad. "I told you, I don't have anything."

"And I told you to shut up," the cop said.

Qasim turned his head the other way, and that's when he saw me. I stopped moving, and me and him locked eyes for a second, and then he looked away.

The police didn't put any handcuffs on Qasim, and they didn't arrest him and take him away in the police car. They just searched him, and when they didn't find anything, the cop that was holding him against the car let him go. Then the cops got back in their car and took off.

The whole thing only lasted, like, two minutes. When the police were gone, Qasim didn't look happy like he always does. His face was hard and tight. He was so mad, this muscle in his jaw was twitching.

He didn't say anything to me. He just started walking up the path to the Center real fast, so fast I had to practically run to keep up with him. "Qasim," I started, but I didn't even know what I was gonna say after that.

I felt embarrassed for him, for what had happened to him in front of everybody. And I felt bad for me, too. I didn't have a whole lot more years before the cops started looking at me, thinking I was doing the wrong thing even when I wasn't.

If that kinda thing could happen to Qasim who was a real good guy, a smart guy that was going to college and everything, then it could definitely happen to a dumb kid like me.

▪ ▪ ▪

I wasn't the only one at the Center who saw what happened to Qasim, and by the time step class started, everybody knew about it. Us guys tried to ask him about it, but Qasim didn't wanna talk.

Terrence came by the Center later in the afternoon. He didn't have to go to work that day, so he came over to run a Man Group. It was a good day for it, too, because we were all as mad as we could get.

Of course the girls wanted to come to Man Group, too. They started whining that they didn't have anything to do and it wasn't fair that we were discriminating against them. Terrence told them that sometimes guys just had to talk by themselves for a while.

When we got in our room and locked the door, we spent a couple minutes searching our room for any girls that might be hiding. Once we were sure it was safe, Terrence handed out a bunch of index cards and we wrote out our questions. I covered my index card with my hand so nobody, I mean *nobody*, would know what I was asking. Then Terrence came around with the shoebox and we dropped our questions inside.

There were only about twelve of us in Man Group that day, so I started getting nervous. I didn't want anyone to know which question was mine because it was too embarrassing.

Terrence pulled out two cards before he got to mine, guys wanting to know how to break up with a girl and how to get their mom to give them more freedom. Then he read my question out loud. "'Do you know if girls can like a boy who is dumber than them?'"

Terrence got a little smile in his face, but then he tried to cover it up. "All girls are different," he said. He put the index card down on the table and looked around the room. The only problem was his eyes stayed on mine a little longer than everybody else's. He probably knew I was the one asking that question.

Of course he knew.

"If you're having trouble in school now, most girls won't hold that against you, just as long as you're trying to improve. Girls, they like when you're trying to be a better man."

A better man. I wondered if Caprice would feel that way about me someday.

"And you know what else?" Terrence laughed. "When I liked a girl, I would ask her if she wanted to study with me. And man, girls loved that. I got my work done, and the girl thought I was serious and intellectual. Win-win situation, you know what I'm saying?"

Some guys laughed, and one of them yelled out, "She kissed you?"

"You know it!" Terrence said, still laughing.

My mind was already wandering away. *Would something like that work for me? Would Caprice ever wanna study with me? And kiss me?*

Terrence started reading another index card, and that brought my mind back to Man Group. " 'What if I like being a boy,' " Terrence read, " 'but I don't like girls?' "

Everyone looked around the room, trying to figure out who wrote that question.

"You don't have anything to worry about," Terrence said. "First of all, y'all are young. What are you guys, eleven, twelve?"

We all nodded.

"When I was your age, I wasn't even thinking about no girls yet. I was into comic books and sci-fi movies. And car magazines. All that stuff. So, man, everybody is different. You might start liking girls next month or next year. It doesn't matter." Then Terrence got serious. "And remember, not every guy is gonna end up liking girls, and that's okay, too. You don't need to like girls to be a good man."

For a few seconds everyone was quiet. I knew what Terrence was talking about. Being different. Most of the time I just wanted to be like everybody else, especially in school. Like, I didn't want anybody knowing how bad I was doing, and even when the teacher asked us if we had any questions, I never raised my hand because I didn't want all the other kids to think I was stupid or something. Being different was hard, no matter what.

At the same time, I still wanted to know who asked that question.

After answering more questions, finally José told Terrence about what happened with Qasim, and that got Terrence to get real serious with us again.

"Let me keep it real with you guys," he said. "When y'all get a little older, you're gonna be stopped by the police. A lot. I been stopped so many times, for nothing. Just because of the way I look, because I'm a black man. The same thing happens to my Puerto Rican and Dominican buddies."

"That's not fair though," Hector said.

"That's racist, man," Kevon called out.

"I know," Terrence said. "It is. And you kids need to do what you can to change things."

I shook my head. "We can't do anything."

"There are a lot of ways to get your voices heard, Jarrett, even as a kid. You can write letters to the mayor, you can protest, you can talk to adults who vote."

"It's not gonna do anything," Ennis said. "The cops always think we're doing the wrong thing. All the time."

"But let me tell you guys something," Terrence said. "In the meantime, till things change, you need to know what to do when you get stopped. Not *if* you get stopped. *When.*"

Me and Kevon looked at each other. I had never seen Terrence like this. What he was telling us was important. I could feel it.

Terrence spent the rest of Man Group telling us how to act when the police stopped us, even when we weren't doing anything wrong. He said we had to keep our mouths closed and only tell them easy things like our names and addresses. If they accused us of anything, the only thing we had to say was, "I would like to call my mom or dad." He said we didn't have to answer anything till we had an adult with us. That was the law, so the police couldn't try to trick us into saying something.

Then we practiced. Terrence played the cop, and we had to show him we knew what to do and wouldn't get mad and give the police any reason to arrest us.

Terrence was serious the whole time. He said what he was telling us was a matter of life and death, and he meant it.

. . .

"I'm gonna go home and take care of the dogs and hang with them for a while," Terrence said to me and Kevon after Man Group was over. "You want me to drop you guys off at home?"

"No," Kevon said. "I wanna shoot some hoops."

"And I need to work on the trailer."

"Alright, guys," Terrence said. "Jarrett, tell your mom I'll be over later."

Me and Kevon walked outta the room together. "You going to the gym?" I asked him, even though that was where he always went.

"Yeah. Some of the guys want me to try out for the basketball team."

"But the caseworkers might find another home for you and —"

"Yeah, I know," he said, and walked away to the gym, like he didn't wanna be bothered.

I didn't follow him. I went the other way, to the video room to work with Lawrence. He only got to work at the Center on Tuesdays and Thursdays, and there was a lot of stuff I had to learn. I had to make sure we would be ready to start shooting the trailer next week, after summer school was over.

"Let me show you this cool new effect," Lawrence said, grabbing a chair and pulling it up to the computer next to me. "This is hype."

For the next hour, he showed me how to make these cool titles, where the words pop on the screen, then change into blood and drip down. It was the best thing I ever saw.

I could have stayed there all night working with the video effects, but I had to get home. The sixth-grade test was on Friday, and I had to be ready for it. I couldn't let anything get in the way again. Not the trailer, not Kevon, not the babies. Nothing.

SIXTEEN

OF COURSE, WHEN I GOT HOME I FOUND OUT WE were getting a new baby that day. Mom was cleaning up and trying to make the caseworkers think our house always looked nice.

I went straight to my room, straight to my desk. I opened my practice book and tried to read one of those long articles about some ship that was in some war or something, but it was really long and I couldn't get into it. So I jumped down to the next article, which was about a woman who invented something *surprising*. But it took too long to get to the surprise, and I knew it was gonna be boring anyway. My mind just couldn't focus on any of it.

So I decided to skip to the vocabulary words because that was something I could learn. I mean, I knew I couldn't learn all of them, but I could learn some.

I opened the book to any ol' page and ended up in the *P* section. The first three words were:

Predicament

Predict

Prejudice

I read the definitions. Then out loud I said, "Why am I in summer school? How did I get myself in this predicament?"

I smiled. Talking to myself was helping me. "I wish I could predict if I was gonna pass this test or not," I said. That wasn't just a vocabulary word. That was the truth.

For the next word, I said, "I wish nobody was prejudice against people who look like me and my friends. Because, then, what happened to Qasim wouldn't happen to anybody else."

"Who you talking to?" I didn't even hear Kevon come into the room.

"Nobody, why?"

"You're mumbling to yourself."

"I'm studying." If I got held back because of Kevon Underwood, I was gonna kill him.

"Your mom said to come and get you for dinner."

"Did the caseworker get here already?"

"Yeah. She left a kid named Hugo."

"Okay." I wanted to do two more words before I closed the book, but I didn't want Kevon standing there while I made up sentences and said them out loud to myself. "You can go now," I told him. Then I stared at him till he left.

When I finished studying, I went to the living room first because I saw Mom and Treasure playing with the new baby. Hugo was probably three years old, and he wasn't quiet like Treasure. This boy was running around laughing and saying, "Catch me! Catch me!"

He was gonna use up a lot of my energy. But first I needed to eat. I was hungry and the food smelled good.

Since Mom was busy in the living room, I made my own plate for dinner, which meant I put the curry chicken and rice on the plate but didn't bother with any vegetables. There was even roti. All of this was food Aunt Inez made and left for us when she was here.

Kevon was sitting at the table, just staring at his plate. "I don't eat this stuff," he said.

"You try it?"

"Don't have to. It looks nasty." And just like that, he got up and walked outta the kitchen, leaving all that food there.

He didn't know what he was missing.

Mom came in and put Treasure in the high chair. Hugo climbed up on the chair next to her. He was smiling, and the next thing I knew, he said, "High five!" and me and him were high-fiving for no reason.

That's when I noticed Hugo had a big bandage wrapped around his chest. I could see it through his T-shirt. "What happened?" I asked my mom, while still high-fiving Hugo.

"B-u-r-n-e-d. Poor little thing spent the last two weeks in the hospital."

I tried to act like what she said didn't bother me because I didn't want Hugo to know we were talking about him. But the little kid got burned, maybe because his mother wasn't paying attention to him or something. That's probably why the caseworkers took him away from her.

After the babies were finished eating, my mom let Treasure outta the high chair and she went running down the hall. Then, without even asking me if I was still hungry, Mom grabbed my plate, put some vegetables on it, and handed it back to me. "Eat," she said.

I just made a grunting noise.

Mom picked up Hugo. "Time for a bath," she said to him, and they left the kitchen.

I was still in the kitchen eating when I heard Mom say kinda loud, "Oh, my goodness. Oh, my goodness."

What was going on?

I ran to the bathroom and stopped dead in my tracks when I saw what she was seeing. The bathtub was already filled with water and bubbles, and she had taken the bandages off Hugo's chest, but she was just frozen, staring.

"Who could do this to their own baby?" she whispered.

By then, I was staring, too. That burn on Hugo's chest — it was an iron. A whole iron with the holes and everything. That was what the burn was shaped like. No way could he do that to himself. Somebody burned him with a hot iron. "Who did that to him?" I asked.

"His mother. She's in j-a-i-l now."

"But why?" I asked, but Mom didn't even try answering my question. There *was* no answer.

I got tears in my eyes looking at that burn. It was a good thing Kevon wasn't around to see me. I just stood there thinking how much that must have hurt, a burn like that.

Mom tried to smile and act like everything was okay, so I did the same thing. I wiped my tears and tried to act normal so Hugo wouldn't think something was wrong.

It was bad, that burn. So hard to look at. And I knew for a

fact, that little boy was gonna have that burn on his chest for the rest of his life.

■ ■ ■

That night, it was hard to stop thinking about Hugo's burn, and so hard to stop being mad. I had helped Mom give Hugo his bath, making sure we didn't get any soap on the burn, and I helped her put new bandages over his chest. The thing about Hugo was, he was always smiling. It was like he didn't know how messed up his world was.

When the bath was over, Mom told me to go back and finish eating, but I couldn't, not after all that. So I threw my food away when she wasn't looking, put my dishes in the sink, and went to my room. It was a long day, seeing what happened to Qasim, then Hugo. I couldn't take any more.

But, of course, there was Kevon in my room with Treasure. "Your mom finished with that other baby?" he asked me. "Because I need to give Treasure a bath."

"Yeah."

"Good."

"My mom can give her a bath, you know."

"I know." He picked up Treasure and left the room with her, and I heard them go in the bathroom anyway.

No matter what, he was gonna do whatever he wanted. But who cared? At least I had my room to myself for a little while.

■ ■ ■

Mom and Terrence got into it again that night, when me and Kevon were already in bed. It wasn't a loud argument or anything, but the second Terrence came home, he said, "Another baby? I thought you were gonna take a break so we could —"

I didn't hear what Mom said back, but then Terrence said, "Remember we were gonna try and go to my friend's cabin for a weekend. Summer's practically over."

Then Terrence reminded Mom that she wanted to go back to college and take some classes, and he asked her how she was supposed to do that if she didn't stop taking babies for a little while.

I couldn't hear her, but I knew what my mom was probably saying. She was saying Hugo needed a place to live, that he was hurt and he needed someone to take care of him. She said that she was gonna go back to college, as soon as she got the chance.

Then they stopped talking, and I thought they made up or something. But in the morning I figured out why everything had gotten so quiet.

Terrence didn't stay over that night. He went back home.

SEVENTEEN

AT THE CENTER THE NEXT DAY, I WALKED INTO the gym and saw Kevon playing basketball with the team. He was wearing the team's uniform, red shorts and a white top, and he had a number on his chest.

In just a week, Kevon was officially on the basketball team. I wondered if he'd told them he wasn't gonna be living here all that long.

The next thing I saw were all the girls that *happened* to be hanging around the gym, watching the boys play. The girls acted like the basketball players were the only boys at the Center. Like the rest of us guys were nothing. The only good thing was that Caprice wasn't there. She wasn't one of those girls giggling over the basketball guys like they had nothing better to do.

Ennis was in the art room working with the little kids. He had the walls covered in thick construction paper and the floor covered with a big drop cloth, and he was teaching the kids how to paint. It looked kinda like they were painting trees and skies and stuff, but it was hard to tell really. He was gonna have to do a lot of work to get those kids to paint something good.

But I went over there anyway, and I told the kids I liked their paintings. Then I asked Ennis, "You see who's on the basketball team?"

"Yeah, of course."

"What's that team gonna think when he's not even here in a couple of days?"

Ennis shrugged. "He's good though."

I didn't wanna hear that. That wasn't the point. Kevon shouldn't have joined the team when he didn't even live around here. I wasn't sure where he lived, but it was probably too far away for him to come here every day for practice and games. What he was doing wasn't right.

I hung out with Ennis for a while, waiting for him to finish with the kids and clean up. Then me and him got out the plaster and worked on some of the props for the movie trailer. We made some weird monster claw hands that were all wrinkly and hairy with long black fingernails.

While they were drying, we walked out into the hall to go to the water fountain. Caprice was out there, holding a clipboard. "Oh, good. You're here, Jarrett," she said. "I need you."

My heart stopped and my brain went dark. I couldn't believe what I was hearing.

Ennis pushed me and I kinda woke back up. "Huh?" I asked.

Caprice came closer to me and showed me what was on the clipboard. It was a sheet of paper that said *Drama Petition*. "I'm trying to get a drama class in the fall. Mrs. Prajapati said she would hire somebody if I get fifteen kids who want to take the class. So, are you in?"

"Drama?" Nothing she was saying was making sense to me.

"Yeah, you know. Acting?"

"I'm not an actor though. I'm a director."

"I know, but this could be fun." She pushed the clipboard closer to me.

"Um, I don't —"

"Please, Jarrett. I only have eight names so far. I need your help." Her face looked so needy and so pretty at the same time.

She needed me.

How was I supposed to say no to that? I took the clipboard and signed my name fast, and then passed it to Ennis. "Not me," he said, throwing his hands in the air. I shot him a dirty look and handed the clipboard back to Caprice.

"Thanks, Jarrett," she said, smiling so cute. Then she looked over my shoulder and ran after some girl. "Alma, wait up!"

I stood there, watching her talk to Alma. I couldn't believe what just happened.

"Did I sign up to be in acting class?" I asked Ennis.

He just laughed.

I shook my head. "This girl. First she has me taking yoga and now acting."

"You're in love," Ennis said.

"Shhh! Don't say that too loud." I looked around, but nobody was near us.

It didn't take long for Caprice to get Alma's name on the list, and then she stood there waiting for someone else. Ennis went to get water, but I just waited till he got back.

"Talk to her," he said.

"I can't. I'm not feeling good."

"But she's alone now. This is your chance."

"I'm gonna do it when I'm ready. Why do you keep pushing me?"

"Because you're lucky."

"Lucky?" What was he even talking about?

He looked down. "I mean, if you like a girl, it's easy to just go over and tell her you like her."

He was just saying that because he didn't like a girl yet. When he did, he would see how hard it really was. Anyway, I didn't like that he was challenging me. "I just talked to her," I told him.

"No, I mean, tell her you like her."

"I told you, I'm feeling kinda weird today," I said.

"You're just trying to get out of talking to the girl you love."

I sighed. "Why don't you talk to Nicole then? If you were with her and I was with Caprice, that would be —"

"I'm not into Nicole. Not like the way you're into Caprice."

I didn't understand Ennis sometimes. *Everybody* liked Nicole. "How can you not like Nicole?"

"*You* don't like her," he said.

"But that's because I like *Caprice*!"

I didn't think Ennis was getting this.

Me and him stood there for another minute, him trying to get me to talk to her, me trying to stall. It was hard, but I didn't know why. Me and her were already kinda like friends. Why couldn't I just tell her how I felt about her already?

I had just taken two steps down the hall in her direction when Nicole ran outta the gym, all glittery in a T-shirt with a giant, shiny gold heart on it. "What are you doing?" she asked Caprice, practically outta breath.

"I'm doing my petition."

Nicole grabbed Caprice's arm. "I've been saving you a seat next to me *forever*! Come watch the boys practice."

Then Nicole practically dragged Caprice back to the gym with her.

I was standing there, wondering what just happened. I mean, I wasn't sure I was gonna be able to do it that time, but maybe I would have been. But now she was gone to watch Kevon and the other *sports* guys.

I had blown my chance. Again.

■ ■ ■

When I got home that night, I closed my door and started going over the tips Mrs. Greer taught us about how to read something and answer questions about it. Then I tried to do some of those boring practice tests, but I still couldn't get through one of them. My brain couldn't do it.

I wished they would let me read the kinda stuff I wanted to read. Like, if I could have read a book about horror movies or something like that, I would do good on all the tests. But teachers never let us read anything good.

A little while later I heard some commotion coming from the living room. Kevon was home, and it sounded like he was mad about something. I opened my bedroom door and heard him saying, "I can put a Band-Aid on my own sister's head. I did it a million times by now."

"Calm down," Mom told him, and that made me fly down the hall to the living room at top speed to see what was going on. Mom was sitting on the couch and Kevon was holding Treasure. "Okay, you can do it," Mom said. "I just want to make sure you clean the area properly."

"I been cleaning her cuts since she was born," Kevon said. He passed me in the hall, carrying Treasure to the bathroom.

Mom sat there, shaking her head. "Treasure had her stitches removed today. Everything healed well, but the doctor wants us to keep the area covered for another few days. I wanted to do it so it would be done right, but —" She didn't have to say any more.

Anyway, I knew she was having a hard time dealing with Kevon. He acted more like he was Treasure's father than her brother.

▪ ▪ ▪ ▪

Terrence came back over that night while I was sitting in the kitchen, eating dinner and trying to study. Mom said she would help me, but she was too busy with the babies, trying to get them to go to sleep. So I was still waiting.

Terrence came into the kitchen. "What's up, man?" he asked, sitting down next to me. He picked up the college catalog Mom left there and smiled. "About time," he said.

"Yeah, I know."

Mom had gone to the college that day to find out about

signing up for some classes, so maybe she was serious about it this time. I hoped so.

Terrence put the book back on the table. "What you doing?"

"Studying."

"You need help? Let's do this, man."

And it was kinda fun, studying, just me and Terrence. He was good at it, too. We ran through a million vocabulary words, and he made me practice reading those passages and writing down the key concepts. Everything was still boring, but every time I felt my mind going somewhere else and I started looking around the room or something, Terrence said, "Focus, Jarrett," and I went back to what I was reading. He said I did okay on the key concepts, too.

I just wished I could have Terrence sitting next to me on Friday, for the big test.

EIGHTEEN

THAT NIGHT, WHILE I WAS SLEEPING, I COULD feel it starting, that heavy weighty feeling right on my chest. I woke up and felt it getting heavier every minute, till I couldn't breathe and I could hardly move. I coughed and coughed and coughed. And every cough hurt more and more.

I reached under my pillow for my inhaler and took a hit. Then another hit. Then another. But it didn't work. I could hardly even get any of the medicine stuff into my body because my lungs weren't working anymore. I was going to die.

Panic took over my brain. I had to get off that bunk bed. I had to get help. *Right away!*

With my last amount of energy, I jumped down off the top bunk, but I was moving so fast, I landed right on my butt. I think it hurt, but I didn't have time to feel it. My time was running out. My chest was burning, and every time I took a breath, I could hear my lungs *groan* like an old car engine.

I had to get help.

I got to my knees real slow, and it took all the strength I had to try to stand up, but I couldn't. I fell back over, just trying to breathe.

"What the heck are you doing?" It was Kevon. He sounded awake but only a little.

I sucked in as much air as possible and tried to say something, but nothing came out. That's when I started panting like a dog. I was still on the floor, on my back, and I couldn't move and I couldn't say anything.

"You probably had a nightmare," Kevon mumbled.

I just panted faster, louder. But no matter what, I couldn't get enough air.

"Hey, what's wrong with you?" Finally, Kevon got outta bed. He stood over me in the dark room. "You okay?"

I shook my head, but I couldn't tell if he saw me.

It took Kevon a few seconds, but then he ran outta the room, and I could hear him banging on my mom's bedroom door. I heard him say real loud, "Ms. Ashby. Ms. Ashby! Jarrett's dying!"

I laid back on the floor, looking up at the ceiling, thinking, *Kevon's right*.

I closed my eyes to die, but then I heard my mom's voice. She was telling Terrence to get my breathing machine, and I heard Kevon say something about calling 911. And then my mom was holding me like I was one of the foster babies and saying something. I knew she was trying to calm me down, but it was hard to calm down since I was too busy dying.

Next thing I knew, my mom was putting me on the breathing machine. She had the mask over my face, and I could hear the machine humming. Terrence was trying to sit me up, and my mom was holding the mask in place. "C'mon, Jarrett," Terrence said. "You can do this. Breathe, man."

I opened my eyes and looked around. My mom was right in front of me and tears were sliding down her face. She was holding the mask with one hand and wiping her face with the other. I couldn't see Terrence, but I could feel him holding my back straight. And Kevon was there, looking scared, walking back and forth and back and forth in front of me.

Then, after a long time, I heard the buzzer ring from downstairs, and Kevon ran outta the room. I was still panting and crying and trying to breathe when the paramedics finally got there. The man and the woman asked Mom a bunch of questions, but my brain was fading out by then. I did hear the man paramedic say, "Ma'am, let us take over now."

They took me off the machine, and they slipped a different plastic mask over my mouth and nose, and the man said something about oxygen. Right away, I could feel my lungs start to open and the air fill me up.

"I'm going to put an IV in your arm, sweetheart," the lady paramedic said, grabbing my arm tight. "Hold still." Half a second later, she stabbed me with a needle.

To be honest, I don't know what happened after that. I was kinda out of it. Not dead because I was breathing in all that oxygen, but definitely only half alive.

Next thing I knew, I was in an ambulance, and Mom was there with me. And I was in a hospital in a room with two other kids on oxygen just like me. But I couldn't hardly stay awake.

■ ■ ■

By the time I felt like I was back to normal, it was already day outside. I was on a hospital bed, but I wasn't in a room really. Just a big place with beds and curtains. Mom was sitting in the chair next to me, watching me sleep or something.

"Mom?" I said.

"How are you doing?" she asked, her eyes getting all teary.

"Better," I said. My throat hurt, but I didn't know why.

"Want some water?"

I nodded, and she poured some water in a plastic cup and helped me drink some of it.

"Do I have — ?" I stopped, rubbed my throat, then tried again. "Do I have to stay here for a long time?"

"No, they just wanted to keep an eye on you overnight, make sure you were okay."

"I'm okay. Can we go home now?"

Mom smiled. "I guess your impatience is a good sign. Let me go find someone to come and check on you."

When she left my bed, I sat up and all the blood ran down from my brain, and I got kinda dizzy. I looked around at all the other sick people I could see from where I was. Most of them were kinda old or, like, *real* old, but across the room I could see another kid, like, a little older than me. He was sleeping and his mom was sitting next to his bed, just like mine was, staring at her son. I wanted to know what he was in here for, and if he was one of the kids who was in the oxygen room with me last night. I couldn't remember.

Actually, I couldn't remember a lot of what happened at all. It was weird what I could remember and what was just, like, missing from my brain.

But there was one thing I definitely did remember:

Kevon saved my life last night.

NINETEEN

WE DIDN'T EVEN HAVE TO OPEN THE FRONT DOOR to hear the noise coming from inside. It sounded like there were, like, thirty kids inside, but no, it was just Treasure and Hugo. At 8:30 in the morning, they were wide awake, running around with towels pinned to their shirts, playing superheroes, I think.

Terrence was standing there, doing play-by-play. "And Hugo runs down the hall with Treasure right behind him. They are saving the world!"

When we stepped inside, he kissed Mom, which was still kinda embarrassing to see. "How you doing, man?" he asked me, patting me on the head like I was one of his dogs, G-Man or Mac.

"I'm better," I said.

That was when I saw Kevon. He was in the kitchen, looking as tired as I was. He was on Terrence's laptop watching a video or something, but he turned around and looked at me. Was I supposed to say something to him? All I could think of was, "Hey."

"Hey," he said back.

And then we were just looking at each other for another few seconds. It was weird. I didn't like that he had this thing over me. "What are you watching?" I asked him.

"This guy that shows you all the cheats, you know, for the games."

"Oh."

Mom put her hand on my back and rubbed it. "Go wash up and brush your teeth," she said. "Then come and lie on the couch."

"But what about summer school?"

"You're not going. You need to rest today."

I was too tired to argue. No, I didn't really wanna go to summer school, but it was the last day before the test, and Mrs. Greer was gonna go over everything and make sure we were ready.

This was the kinda thing that happened all the time to me. Every time I had a bad asthma attack, I had to stay home from school for a day or two, and then when I went back, I never knew what they were doing. In sixth grade, I missed sixteen days. All because of stupid asthma.

▪ ▪ ▪

I kinda didn't wanna go back to school the next day, but I had to. I had to take the stupid sixth-grade test. Again.

If I thought I was gonna fail it before, now I was positive because yesterday was a total waste and I didn't get to study at all.

In the morning, before I left for school, Terrence told me to do my best, that I couldn't change anything now. He said all I could do was try.

So that's what I did. I tried . . . well, at first anyway. I sat there for all those hours, and I answered the questions I knew. Some of it wasn't too hard, not for me. But then I got to where you had to read that long, boring stuff about history or some person you never heard of, and you had to answer questions about it, and that's where everything fell apart for me. I knew the words, but I couldn't read the words and think about the story at the same time. It had to be one or the other.

That's when I decided to forget everything Terrence told me. I was done trying.

So, right there, I stood up, grabbed my backpack, and walked over to Mrs. Greer's desk. I could feel all the other boys looking at me, probably wondering what I was doing. But I didn't care.

"Is everything okay?" Mrs. Greer whispered to me.

"It's fine, ma'am." I handed her my test papers.

"What's going on?"

"I'm leaving," I said.

"Leaving? We still have" — she looked at her watch — "forty-two minutes left."

"I'm done." I walked to the door with everybody's eyes on me.

Mrs. Greer stood up. "Jarrett, if you leave this room, you can't come back. Those are the rules."

I shrugged. "Okay."

"And you can't leave the school."

I stopped and turned around. "Why not?"

"We need to call your mother if you want to leave early. You have to go to Mr. Johnson's office right now."

"Okay." I opened the door.

"Jarrett, last chance. Are you sure you don't want to finish your test?"

"I'm sure," I said. "You were right, Mrs. Greer. I'm stupid."

▪ ▪ ▪

Mr. Johnson was behind his big principal's desk when I went in. He was on his computer writing something, and all he did was take his hand and point to the chair. So I sat there waiting for him to yell at me.

It took him a few minutes before he said, "Why aren't you taking your exam, Mr. Crawford?"

I sat back in the seat and shrugged.

"You must have an answer," he said. "You're an intelligent young man who should be able to express himself."

"I'm not intelligent, sir. But you already know that because I heard Mrs. Greer tell you that last week. You already know how dumb I am."

I could tell Mr. Johnson was surprised because his eyes got wide but only for half a second. Then he tried to act cool. "This is a school for young men. Honorable men. What you did, eavesdropping on a private conversation, was not honorable, Mr. Crawford."

He was trying to make me feel bad, but that didn't change what I heard.

He went on. "Yes, Mrs. Greer was concerned about you, Jarrett. You've fallen behind, and this has been going on for the past few years according to your records."

"I miss a lot of school," I said.

"Yes, you do. But you are also struggling with reading, and this will not get better unless you get help."

I didn't wanna hear this. I just wanted to get up and walk outta there and go home. "I don't wanna do sixth grade again," I told him.

"Well, we don't know if you passed or not, so let's wait until we have those results before making any decisions. Either way, Mr. Crawford, think about coming here in the fall. I started this charter school to work with boys just like you."

"You mean dumb boys?"

"That's *not* what I mean." Mr. Johnson stood up from behind his desk. "Did I tell you I grew up right here in Newark? I was a lot like you. Single mother, hardworking. Always just getting by."

I looked down. Now he was gonna tell me his whole life story. I would rather be taking the test than listening to this.

"I was one of those kids who always got in trouble. Not bad. Bored. I didn't know what to do with myself, you know? By the time I was fifteen, I had served three months in juvenile detention."

I sat forward in my seat and looked up at him. "You?"

"Yeah. Dumbest thing I ever did. Changed my life though."

"How?"

"Scared me. The boys in that place were some tough dudes. I *thought* I was tough, but I wasn't like those guys, and I didn't want to be. I had to get myself together. Change, you know? And it wasn't easy."

Mr. Johnson kept talking, telling me about how hard it was to finish high school in his neighborhood, how the guys he used to hang out with would make fun of him and fight him because he was trying to do the right thing. Then when he finished high school, he went away to college. He didn't wanna stay in Newark. He thought he would go away to college and never come back.

"But here I am," he said. "Back in Newark." He laughed — the first time I ever saw Mr. Johnson laugh.

"My friend wants me and him to go to college together," I said, and I couldn't help thinking that if I got held back, Ennis would always be a year ahead of me. We wouldn't be able to go to college together no matter what.

"You can do it," Mr. Johnson said. "If I can, you can."

"Not if I don't get outta sixth grade."

"I had to repeat fifth," he said. "And I had to go to summer school to pass tenth."

"For real?"

He nodded. "Same problem. Reading. It took me a long, *long* time to like reading. Now I have a lot of books to catch up on."

"I'm never gonna like reading," I said. "It's boring and dumb. Movies are better than books anyway."

"I wish you could give our school a chance to change your mind about that, Jarrett," Mr. Johnson told me. "I don't want you to get the way I got when I was your age. By then, I had already given up on school and myself. Think about coming here. We have a long waiting list, but I know the guy in charge."

A waiting list? To come to a corny all-boys school with no girls?

I didn't get that.

■ ■ ■

By the time Mr. Johnson let me outta school, I wasn't in the mood to go to the Center. There are days when you wanna have fun, and days when you know nothing is gonna make you happy. This was the second kinda day.

Only, I couldn't just go home and sit in my room being miserable like I was planning to do. No, nothing was working out for me that day. Because a half a block from my house, I ran into Mom, Treasure, Hugo, and Rafa walking down the street, all holding hands with one another.

"Perfect timing," Mom said, and something told me that running into them wasn't really an accident. "We're on our way to the drugstore, just for a minute so I can return a lipstick. Then we're all going to the park. Come with us." She tried to smile, but it didn't work. She looked more sorry for me than anything else.

Just what I needed. Pity.

"Mom, I don't feel like it," I said. "Can I just go home?"

"Come on. I could use some help with these three."

I knew she was trying to cheer me up, but nothing was gonna work.

"I'm tired," I said.

"We won't be there long. I'm just trying to wear them out so they can take a long nap."

I sighed. There was no getting outta this. I could tell.

We walked down to the corner, and when it was time to cross the street, Treasure grabbed my hand. And her little baby hand stayed in mine all the way to the store and all the way to the park. No matter how bad I messed up in summer school, she still liked me.

"Mr. Johnson called," Mom said as we walked into the park.

"I know. I was right there when he called."

"So, you didn't do well?"

I wasn't sure if she was asking or telling me. "Nah."

"You tried your best, Jarrett. You can't do more than that."

Did I really try my best? I wasn't sure about that.

We walked in the direction of the little kid area. Mom used to take me there when I was little so I could play with whatever foster brother or sister I had at the time.

Treasure pulled on my hand to make me walk faster. She was practically running to get to the play area.

As soon as we got there, she let go of my hand and ran over and climbed on this fake turtle thing with Hugo and Rafa.

Hugo got to the top first, and he tried to stand up. "Don't fall, baby," Mom yelled.

She always told me the same thing. Don't fall. But here I was, not a baby anymore, and I was falling flat on my face.

While my mom played with the kids, helping them climb on more animals, I sat on the bench, watching. Thinking. The whole park didn't make any sense. Why would they make the turtle, the lion, and the giraffe all the same size?

But that's not what I was thinking about. I was thinking about my life and what a disaster it was.

I didn't even notice Treasure till she literally climbed on my lap and stuck her finger in my chin.

"Ow."

She laughed at my pain.

"Go back and play with the boys," I told her. "I'm thinking."

She didn't move.

"I said, go back, Treasure." I didn't mean to get mad at her, but I wasn't in the mood to play.

That's when she did it. That little baby slapped me, right across the face. For real.

"What?" I picked her off me and put her back on the ground. Then I stood up and looked down on her. "You can't hit people, Treasure."

Mom came over and picked her up. "Don't hit," she told her, a little too late. Then she said to me, "She didn't mean it, Jarrett. Kids like her, who don't speak, they sometimes don't know any other way to express themselves. She wants you to play with her."

"I know, but I told her no. And just because she can't talk, that doesn't mean she doesn't understand every single word we're saying because she does."

"Play with her for a little while," Mom said. "It'll take your mind off your problems."

I took a deep breath and tried not to be mad, especially at Treasure. It took about ten breaths for me to finally stop being 100 percent mad and only be about 83 percent mad. "Okay, Treasure," I said after a while. "Let's go."

Mom put her down, and she ran over and grabbed my hand. I took her over to the baby swing and buckled her into the little bucket seat. I pushed her, slow at first and then a little faster, but she didn't get scared. So I pushed her higher. I would have kept going if Mom didn't tell me to stop, to give her a rest. So I took her out, and she ran back over to the boys. I went back over to the bench.

This time Mom sat down next to me. "These kids are wearing me out," she said to me, even though her eyes never left the little baby slide. "I brought them here so they would take a nap later, but I'm the one who's going to need one."

"You should be a teacher," I told her. "Like, for little kids."

"Thanks, Jarrett. That's nice to hear. I wanted to be a teacher, back when I was young, in college. But, you know, things changed."

"You mean *I* changed things."

She put her arms around me. "You were the best thing that ever happened to me. You changed things for the better."

Yeah, right.

"Terrence has been trying to get me to go back to college and get my degree, but it's going to be hard, even though they have online classes now that I can do from home. But I don't know if I'll have a free moment, not with all the babies."

"You can stop taking the babies," I said. "I mean, just till you finish college."

"Now you sound like Terrence."

"He's right."

"I know," she said. "But I love these kids so much."

We sat quietly for a while, just watching the babies go down the slide over and over again. They never got bored with it.

"So, the test?" Mom said. "It was really hard?"

"Yeah. I didn't know anything."

"Well, let's wait and see how you did."

"I failed," I said. "I quit before it was over."

Mom sighed. "Okay, let's talk about everything after we get the test results. But if you don't pass, I know I don't want you going back to your school in September. There are other options. Maybe you need something different, Jarrett."

Something different. Couldn't she see my whole life was something different all the time? I couldn't take any more different right now.

But that wasn't the way things worked, not for me. Things always changed. Always.

TWENTY

I COULDN'T WAIT FOR ENNIS TO GET TO MY HOUSE on Saturday. I had stressed out the whole night, worrying about the test and how bad I messed up, so I was ready to work on something I actually knew how to do, the movie trailer.

Kevon had basketball practice that day, and when he got back, he went to my room and passed out on the bed. Practice must have been harder than he thought it would be. He was sleeping with his mouth open and everything.

I opened the trunk and pulled out the tarp and the paint and the masks that weren't 100 percent finished yet. On my way down the hall, I heard Mom on the phone ordering pizza. Yes! Aunt Inez had taken Treasure and Hugo shopping with her, so while I set up everything in the living room I didn't have to deal with kids running around for a change. The pizza was delivered about two minutes after Ennis got there. It smelled good, too.

"I hope you boys are hungry," Mom said. "I got a large pie for the three of you."

"I'm not hungry, Ms. Ashby," Ennis said. "My mom cooked one of my favorite things."

"Oh, no," I said, backing up. "What did she make?"

Ennis grinned. *"You'll find out."*

My heart started beating louder. Panic.

"What are you two boys talking about?" Mom asked.

"Nothing, Ms. Ashby."

But it was something. Something bad.

"Okay, well, boys. If you get hungry, the pizza is here. And I bought some cookies and chips and —" Mom's cell phone rang. "Oh, that's Terrence. We're going to dinner and then the movies. I'll be back in the morning. Don't destroy the living room." She answered the phone and told him she was on the way downstairs.

"Where were you yesterday and Thursday?" Ennis asked me after Mom left. "You weren't at the Center. These two girls got into a fight yesterday and —"

"I had a real bad asthma attack, and I had to go to the hospital. In an ambulance."

Ennis's eyes got real wide. "For real?"

I nodded. "Yeah, I almost, like, died or something." I didn't wanna tell him anything more, especially anything about Kevon and how he might be the reason I was still alive.

"Did you make it to school for the test?"

"Yeah."

"And?"

I shook my head.

"Hard?"

"Yeah. I messed up. I don't think I'm gonna —"

"Don't say it," Ennis warned. "Think positive, okay?"

That was another reason me and Ennis were friends. He knew the right thing to say to me when I was just about to get really down on myself, the way I had all night. Just kicking myself for giving up.

"Okay, let's work," I said. And for the next two hours straight we focused on what we had to do to be ready. I wrote out a list of all the scenes I needed to shoot while Ennis finished painting the last three masks. They looked cool. Every mask was a little different, but you could tell they were all from the same monster family.

I was done before he was, so I reached into his backpack for the little sketchbook. "Did you draw anything new?"

Before I could get my hands on that book, he got to it first. "Nothing good."

"Can I see?"

"No, not yet." Then he got kinda quiet and kept painting.

Something was going on with him, and I didn't know why he wasn't telling me what it was.

"Ennis," I began, "do you, um, are you writing in a diary now?"

Ennis looked up at the ceiling for a second. "Not a diary. That's what girls write in. I have a *journal*."

"Oh." A few seconds went by, and then I figured out what I wanted to ask him. "What kinda stuff are you writing about?"

He shrugged. "I don't know. Stuff I'm thinking about. You know, like, my thoughts."

I nodded, trying to get what he was saying, but what kinda

thoughts was Ennis having? Did he really have enough thoughts for a whole book?

"Ever since you went to Jamaica and came back, you're acting different," I said to him. "I mean, you're still the same, but you're kinda different, too."

"That doesn't make any sense," Ennis said.

"You know what I mean."

"Yeah, but . . . forget it." There was something he wasn't telling me. He was keeping secrets.

"Just tell me what's going on," I said. "We're supposed to be best friends, like, for real."

For, like, a minute, a whole minute, Ennis didn't say anything.

I watched him paint for a little while, but the weird thing was, he wasn't talking like he always did.

"What's the matter with you?"

"Nothing."

"You're not gonna tell me about Jamaica or anything?"

"Nah, I'm tired of all that stuff."

Whoa, that was new. "Since when?"

"Since forever."

"Last week you said everything about Jamaica was better than here. Now you're —"

"Forget about what I said. I didn't mean it."

Okay. I opened Terrence's laptop to look at the script, and Ennis went back to painting. I waited for him to say something, tell me what was going on and why everything changed, but it took a long time.

Finally, he said, "I don't want to go back next summer. It's a waste of time, when I could be here working on a movie with you."

"Okay," I said. "But what about your dad? Don't you wanna see him?"

"Not really."

"Why?"

He shook his head. "He doesn't really care about me. When I was there . . ." He stopped. "Forget it."

I closed the laptop. "Come on, Ennis. Tell me. I won't tell anybody."

He looked down. "My dad, he treats me okay. Fine. But every time we went somewhere with his friends, they were all saying stuff about me. Bad stuff."

"Like what?" I couldn't think of anything bad someone could say about Ennis. He was nice to everybody.

"They said stuff like my father should make me come and live with him because I didn't act right, like, I wasn't doing the kinda stuff boys are supposed to do. And my dad, he didn't even say anything to them. He wasn't on my side, you know?"

I nodded.

"When it's just me and him, everything is fine, but every time other people are around, he thinks I'm not, like, okay or something."

"That's crazy," I said. I tried to think what those other guys meant when they said he didn't act right. What else was he supposed to be doing?

Me and Ennis talked some more, but really, what was I supposed to tell him? I didn't know how to talk about fathers.

Finally, Ennis asked, "You ready to watch the movie?"

"Yeah. Let's do it!" I think both me and him needed to go back to having some fun.

"Go get Kevon," he said.

"Oh, man. Why did you have to remind me?" Ennis was right though. There was no getting outta it. I couldn't leave Kevon by himself all night.

Down the hall, I actually thought about knocking on my room door, but no way was I gonna start doing that when it was *my* room, not *our* room. So I just opened the door and real fast Kevon jumped up from off the floor with his back to me. Then I saw him stick something into the side pocket of his backpack and push it all the way down. I couldn't see what it was, not from where I was standing, but it was black and shiny.

"What are you doing?" I asked, still standing in the door.

Kevon turned around, looking guilty. Very guilty. Then he lied and said, "Nothing," like I was gonna believe that. "What, you spying on me now?"

"No, I was — I was coming to see if you wanted to watch a movie with us, but if you don't —"

"Alright," he said. "There's nothing else to do. Any more pizza left?"

"Yeah, a lot."

I looked around my room fast, scanning everything to see if anything was missing. But I had so much stuff, so many little things that there were a ton of things he could have taken, stuff I wouldn't even know was missing till he was long gone from here.

"I'm starving," he said, zipping the side pocket. He was definitely hiding something in there. He better not have stolen anything from me because that would be it. No way was I gonna live with a thief.

I eyed that backpack again, then looked away fast. Kevon didn't know it, but I was gonna find out what was in that bag.

I ran back down the hallway. Ennis was in the kitchen getting some more Crystal Light. I leaned close to him and whispered, "He's hiding something."

"Who?" Of course Ennis spoke too loud. That guy didn't have a spy bone in his body.

"Shhh. I'm talking about —" I moved my eyes dramatically in the direction of my room. Then I went back to whispering. "He has something, but he hid it in his backpack as soon as I came in the room."

"So what?"

"So . . . What do you mean? He's in my room. I have a right to know what he's hiding. He might be stealing from me for all I know."

"What if he's not stealing from you?"

"That's the point. I have to find out."

Kevon came down the hall and headed straight for the kitchen and the pizza. "No pepperoni?"

"No," I told him. "I got sausage because that's what Ennis liked, but he's not hungry."

Kevon grabbed a slice. "How can you not be hungry for pizza?"

"My mom cooked," Ennis said, and for the second time I waited for him to say more, to tell us what he ate, but he still wasn't giving up any details.

It didn't take long for us to find out though. A little while later, when the movie was playing and we were laying on the floor all over the living room, I heard it. And it was loud, kinda like there was an animal growling right there in the room. Before my brain could even figure out what was happening, it hit me, right in the face. Hard. "Aargh!" I screamed, jumping up.

Kevon jumped up, too. "What — ?"

"Oh, no," I screamed. "No, no!"

Ennis started laughing.

"What *is* that?" Kevon asked.

"It's curry goat!" I screamed. Ennis had just let loose the loudest, deadliest, curry-goatyist fart in the world.

"I had two plates." He was still laughing. "It was good, too."

I couldn't even stay in the living room anymore. It was that bad. And I knew Ennis. He would be blasting all night.

I ran down the hall into my room and closed the door behind me fast before the smell got there, too. I wasn't worrying about Kevon being stuck out there with Ennis. I had to save myself.

Two seconds later, Kevon ran into the room and slammed the door behind him. "It's bad out there," he said, breathing hard.

"Who are you telling? When he eats his mom's curry goat, I don't know what happens in his body, but it's horrible. Takes forever to air out, too."

"That dude needs to go see a doctor," Kevon said.

Me and him sat on the bottom bunk together for a while, just trying to breathe in as much good air as we could. I just hoped the smell wouldn't come in under the door or something.

There was a knock on the door. "Oh, no," Kevon said.

"If that's Ennis, I —"

The door opened, but it wasn't Ennis. It was Aunt Inez and she didn't look happy. "Lawd ah Mercy, boys. You know what time it is?" Whenever she was mad, her Guyanese accent got thicker and thicker. "Running up and down, back and forth, and slamming doors. What is wrong with you?"

"Sorry, Aunt —"

"You want to wake up them babies?"

"No, Aunt —"

"Don't talk back, boy."

"But I didn't —"

"You boys need to settle down," Aunt Inez said. "No more running up and down the hall. If you're going to be in here, turn off the TV in the living room."

"But we're watching a —"

"Then go in there and watch it. You got that TV blasting and you're in here. You think your mother has money to waste on electricity if —" She kept talking as she walked back down the hall to my mom's room and closed the door. Mom says Aunt

Inez likes to fuss, but I just call it complaining out loud to nobody.

Me and Kevon waited a little while longer, just to give the living room a chance to clear out some of that rotten air. Good thing we had opened the window wide when we were painting the masks. By the time we slowly went back out there, the living room still stank, but we weren't choking anymore.

Ennis laughed when he saw us. "I thought you were strong men," he said.

Kevon shook his head. "Not *that* strong."

I jumped back on my sleeping bag, which was closest to the window just by luck. "Start the movie again," I told Ennis.

"Wait a second," Kevon said. "I need to get another slice." He ran into the kitchen.

Ennis looked at me. "Are you still gonna — ?"

"Shhh." I looked over my shoulder. "Don't let me go to sleep. I'm gonna wait for him to fall asleep and then do what I have to do." I knew I was sounding way more dramatic than I needed to, but a spy mission was a spy mission, even if it was just to my own room.

■ ■ ■

By the time the movie was over, and the screen went completely dark, I sat up and looked around the room. I should have known the room was too quiet. Both Ennis and Kevon were out cold.

I got up as quietly as possible and moved across the living room without making any noise at all. Then I went down the hall really slow, back to my room, and closed the door silently. So far so good.

My heart was racing when I opened the side pocket of Kevon's backpack and grabbed that shiny object he was trying to hide from me. But even before I pulled it out, I knew what it was. A phone.

The room was dark and I didn't wanna turn the light on, so I zipped the pocket back up, and flew outta the room with the phone. The only place where I could lock the door and turn on the lights was the bathroom, so I went in there. I needed time to examine that phone and find out if Kevon was calling someone or if somebody was calling him.

It took me a few minutes to figure out how to check his call history. The last call made was to 911 and that was from almost two weeks ago, on the night he came here. Kevon must have needed help. Maybe that was when Treasure got hurt. He hadn't made any calls since he'd gotten here, and nobody had called him. And there weren't any messages either.

Then I saw why. While I tried to find some more information, I got a message on the screen that said there were no minutes left on the phone, that they had expired two days ago. Kevon would have to buy a phone card if he wanted to call somebody.

So Kevon had this phone, but he never tried calling anyone. And now he couldn't because he didn't have any money for a new card. So what had he been doing when I came into the room?

And why was he hiding the phone all this time?

■ ■ ■

I got back on top of my sleeping bag and tried to get comfortable, but it was hard. I ended up on my back, looking up at the ceiling while my mind raced again, trying to figure out what Kevon was up to.

I was still thinking of all the possibilities when I heard, "So, you're gonna do it?" It was Ennis, and he sounded half asleep.

"Shhh." What was the matter with him? Was he trying to get me caught or something? I whispered as low as I could, "I did already."

"No, I mean, Caprice. Are you gonna talk to her next week?"

Why was he bringing that up again now? "I don't know," I whispered back. "I'm trying, alright."

"Try harder. Summer is almost over."

I took a deep breath and laid there on the floor, looking up at the ceiling. He was right. My time was running out. I needed to know if she liked me before I found out if I had to do sixth grade over.

"You like Caprice?" Now it was Kevon. He was awake and probably listening to everything we said. "I didn't know you liked her," he said, sitting up. "You never told her?"

"No, I —"

"He's scared," Ennis said. "I keep telling him to get it over with already."

"I can help you," Kevon said. "I know how to talk to girls and get them to like you. I had a girlfriend last year."

"You did?" I asked, sitting up, too. "An actual girlfriend?"

"Yeah. But we broke up. She wasn't, you know, my type."

I wasn't sure if I had a type or not, but if I did, Caprice was it.

"If you want this girl in your life," Kevon said, "you have to start letting her know you're ready for a girlfriend. You have to take care of yourself, Jarrett. Look good. Smell good. That's what girls like."

I nodded. "Yeah, that makes sense." I bet I was gonna have to finally do something about my toenails, too. But I was willing to go that far for the girl I loved.

"I'll show you my routine," Kevon said. "Don't worry about anything. When I'm done with you, Caprice is going to beg you to be her boyfriend."

"Okay," I said.

I laid back down on the sleeping bag and looked up at the ceiling again. Only this time, I had a smile on my face.

TWENTY-ONE

ON MONDAY MORNING, MY WHOLE ROOM SMELLED nasty, like underarms and burning garbage. "What *is* that?" I asked Kevon.

"Musk oil," he said. "Girls like it." He was smiling at himself in the mirror and rubbing more of that oil on his neck, stinking up the whole room.

"You're using too much of that stuff," I told him. "God!"

"You don't know anything because you're not even a teenager yet."

"You're not a teenager either," I said. "You're only a little bit older than me."

"Old enough to be growing a mustache."

I stared at his face in the mirror. "A mustache? You're joking, right?"

"I said *growing*. It's not out yet, but I can feel it coming in under my skin. It itches."

I stared directly at him. "You're dreaming."

"Believe whatever you want." He didn't even look at me. He was putting some kinda grease in his hair, which was already too oily. "Just wait. My mustache is gonna be here in about a week. Then the girls are gonna be all over me."

I started laughing. There was something wrong with him. He needed a psychiatrist or something.

"Don't laugh," he said. "I'm serious." He kept staring in the mirror and trying to make himself look good. "I thought you wanted Caprice to like you."

"I do, but —"

"How long you been into her anyway?"

"Not that long," I lied. "Just a couple weeks — like, fourteen or twenty weeks. Forget I even said anything."

"Shut up," Kevon said. "I'm gonna help you."

He grabbed me and pulled me in front of the mirror. "If you want Caprice to like you, you'll do everything I just did." He pointed to the little musk oil bottle and the jar of grease on the dresser. "Learn from the master."

He left the room, walking away like he was famous. As soon as he left, I opened the bottle, put a little musk oil on my finger, and rubbed it on my neck. Then I put on a little more.

I wasn't gonna put on as much as he did though. I didn't have to. I didn't want *every* girl at the Center to love me. Just one.

I slapped some grease in my hair, too, and rubbed it in good. If Kevon was right, if girls liked this nasty smell and greasy hair, I guess it couldn't really hurt me any.

■ ■ ■

Me and Kevon walked into the Center that day smelling the same, with our heads shining the same. Kevon went to the gym for basketball, and I went to the art room to find Ennis. He was writing in his little black sketchbook again, but this time he didn't try to hide it from me. He did close it though.

"What are you doing?" I asked him even though it was obvious.

He stood up. "Waiting for you." He stuck the sketchbook in his back pocket.

"You draw the flyers?"

"Yeah, here." On the other table he had the flyer already finished on a sheet of construction paper:

☆ AUDITIONS TODAY ☆

ACTORS WANTED

COME TO ROOM 112 AT 11:00 TO TRY OUT FOR A ROLE IN A HORROR MOVIE TRAILER. YOU CAN BE A MONSTER OR A VICTIM. WE NEED DEAD BODIES, TOO.

NO PAY.

All around the page, Ennis had drawn little pictures of all kinds of monsters with veins on their faces and black, scary-looking eyes. "Cool," I said. "Everybody's gonna wanna be in our trailer. You're the best artist in the world."

Me and Ennis went to the office and they let us make ten copies of the flyer on colored paper. Then we split up so we could hang them up around the Center where we knew people would see them.

▪ ▪ ▪

It took me and Ennis a while to set up the room for the auditions. I put up three giant sheets of paper on the walls. On the first one I wrote *MONSTERS*, and I made some lines so everyone who wanted to audition for a monster part could write their names. I put a lot of lines because I knew everyone was gonna wanna be a monster. If I wasn't the director, that's what I would have wanted to be. On the other two sign-up sheets, I wrote *VICTIMS* and *DEAD BODIES*.

Ennis brought some of the masks into the room so the monsters could try them on when they auditioned. Nobody was gonna wanna be a victim once they saw those masks.

"We should audition the victims and dead people first," I told him. "And let's hide the masks till that's done."

"Good idea," Ennis said. He took the masks and put them in one of the filing cabinets where nobody would find them.

Kevon came into the room. "Y'all ready?"

I looked around. "Yeah, I think so."

"I heard some kids out there talking about it."

"Are you gonna audition?" Ennis asked him.

"Can't. I got basketball practice in an hour and tomorrow when y'all are shooting. But I would have been the star of this movie, if I could. I'm a good actor."

"You think you're good at everything," I said.

"I am though."

"You could be a corpse," Ennis said. "That won't take long, and you won't have to miss practice."

"Cool," Kevon said. And before I could stop him, he was taking the Sharpie and signing his name on the *DEAD BODIES* sign-up sheet. "You're gonna see some good dead-guy acting. Watch."

Thirteen guys showed up for the audition. Most of them were from the step team, but some younger kids showed up, too, which was good because we needed more victims for the monsters to attack. And those kids would make easy targets.

Next we did the dead bodies, which really went fast and was the most quiet audition in the world. This one kid, James, he couldn't do it for anything. Every time he tried to lay there and not move, he would start itching or laughing. So I made him an extra, just a kid walking down the street.

Then we cast the monsters, which all went to the guys from the step team, mostly because they were the biggest. The only step guy who didn't get a monster part was José. He was the funniest kid I knew, and I didn't wanna waste him under a mask. He needed to be the lead actor.

Right before we were almost finished, my skateboarder friend Yu showed up. "You're here!" I knew I sounded way too excited, not cool at all, but Yu was just the guy I needed for the movie. Everything was perfect now.

I pulled José next to Yu and looked at the two of them together. It would work.

"Okay, José, you and Yu, y'all are brothers," I said.

José looked over at Yu. "Me and him? Brothers?"

A couple of guys started laughing, and I had to admit, they couldn't look any more different. But I didn't wanna say that to them. "You're supposed to be actors," I told him. "Remember?"

"Actors?" José asked. "Is he supposed to *act* Puerto Rican or am I supposed to *act* Chinese?"

"Look, José," I said, "You wanna be in this or not?"

"Yeah, but —"

"I'm the director. You and him are brothers, okay?"

José shrugged. "Whatever you say, Mr. Director Man."

"Good." When it came down to it, I couldn't have actors taking over my trailer. I was the one who was in charge.

"Okay, everyone," I said to the whole group of actors. "We're gonna be shooting tomorrow and Thursday, beginning at ten." We could only shoot when Lawrence was there with the expensive video camera. "Don't be late. Another thing, don't tell anyone what the trailer is about. I wanna surprise everyone when we show it at the block party."

"Yes, Mr. Director Man," I heard, but this time it was Yu who said it.

"Auditon's over," I yelled, even though they were already on the way outta the door.

When everyone left, me and Ennis took the sign-up sheets down and packed up the masks.

"You happy with the cast?" he asked me.

"Yeah. You?"

He nodded. "But next time, let's do a real movie."

I didn't say anything. Sometimes I think Ennis didn't know me at all. Did he really think someone like me could write and direct a whole movie? He was smart, but me? I didn't think I could ever do something like that.

I saw Caprice in the hall, and for the first time in a long time, she was by herself, not with a bunch of other girls and not with a clipboard. This was it, my chance to talk to her.

I was looking and smelling good that day, so what could be better? I would never get her alone while I was looking this handsome again.

So I did it. I walked up to her and said, "Hey." It was all I could think of, and I was feeling kinda proud of myself about it.

"Jarrett. Are you coming to yoga today?"

Yoga. I'd forgotten all about that. "Yeah, of course. I would never miss yoga."

She smiled. I wanted to just look at her, but my mind went to my feet and how I forgot to wash them and cut my toenails. They were probably gonna be smellier and more clawlike than last week.

But I had to focus on what I was doing. I was gonna tell her I liked her, ask her if she liked me, and then I was gonna ask her to be my girlfriend. And by the time I got home, I was gonna be the happiest guy in Newark.

"Caprice, I have something, um, I wanna tell you . . ." I looked down at the ground and took some quick breaths. I could feel my head getting light and dizzy, and I hoped I wouldn't have another asthma attack right there in front of her.

"Jarrett?"

"Um." I looked back up at her, and the words came outta my mouth before I knew what I was saying. "Would you like to be in my movie trailer? I have a great part just for you."

What was I talking about?

Caprice smiled so big you would have thought she'd won a big acting award or something. "Are you serious?"

"Um, yeah, I mean, yeah." I sounded like an idiot. I knew it, but I couldn't stop it from happening.

"That's gonna be so much fun. I love acting." She actually jumped a little bit off the ground. "Can Nicole be in it, too? We do everything together."

"Yeah, she can be in it. But you, you're gonna be one of the stars."

"Oh, my God. Thanks, Jarrett. Let me go tell Nicole." She ran down the hall to the cafeteria.

I walked in the same direction, slower. Ennis was sitting at one of the tables, with his sketchbook open in front of him. I still didn't see any pictures though, just a bunch of words, and he closed it when he saw me coming. I sat down.

"I tried to do it," I said. "You know, tell her."

He leaned forward and whispered. "And?"

"And I gave her a part in the trailer."

"Is she gonna be a dead body?"

"No, I told her she could have one of the starring roles."

Ennis's eyes got bigger. "What? We don't have any parts for girls."

"We have to rewrite the script. Tonight."

"*You* have to do it," he said. "That's what you get for changing things without asking me. I thought we were partners."

"We are, but this is about love, man. *Love*."

Ennis didn't understand. Sometimes a guy had to do big things for the girl he loved.

TWENTY-TWO

WE HAD THE FIRST DAY OF SHOOTING THE NEXT day, outside behind the Center, close to the Dumpsters, where our monsters lived.

There were so many actors there, and so many other kids watching, it was hard to hear myself think. Directing was almost impossible. I wished I had one of those megaphones directors walked around with so I could tell my actors what I wanted them to do without having to yell, but there was no money in the budget for anything like that.

Instead I had to scream. "Okay, everyone! We're gonna do one rehearsal and then we're gonna get in costume and do it for real. Okay?"

Working with these actors wasn't easy. They took so long learning what to do, I was starting to lose my mind with them. And the story was so simple: These real scary bloody monsters with boogers dripping outta their noses are terrorizing the neighborhood. They sneak up on José and Yu as they're skateboarding in the parking lot, surround them, and then snatch Yu. Nobody believes José when he tries to tell them what's happening. They think Yu just ran away or something. Finally,

Caprice and Nicole believe him and they all look for Yu. But then the monsters surround them, too. And all we hear is Caprice screaming and screaming.

Then the title was gonna come up on the screen: *Terror in the Hood*. The words were gonna drip down in blood.

Lawrence was there while we were shooting, making sure I held the camera steady, which was harder than before because this camera was heavy. And Ennis was writing down all the shots the way Lawrence taught us how to, so that it would be easy to find the clips we wanted to use in the final trailer.

We worked for almost three hours and then some of the little kids had to go to soccer practice. And even with all the actors messing up and laughing when they were supposed to be scared, it was still a lot of fun. It felt so good telling everyone what to do and making sure they did it the way I wanted. Most of all, I really liked being good at something.

■ ■ ■

We had a free morning at the Center the next day, so all of us guys just hung out in the gym, not playing a real game or anything, but just running around and acting stupid. The girls were there, too, but they were over on the other side of the gym, playing music and dancing. I wished we could have worked on the movie, so at least I would have a reason to talk to Caprice again, but we couldn't because Lawrence wasn't there on Wednesdays.

At the same time, it was fun just hanging out, not doing

anything. After six weeks in summer school, this was what summer was supposed to be about.

I would have just hung out all day, but right after Miss Lisa came and told us to line up for lunch, I saw something outta the corner of my eye.

It was Kevon. And, even though he was trying to be smooth about it, he was sneaking outta the Center.

I don't know what happened to me, but it was like the spy part of my body jumped into action before I could stop it. I had to follow him. I had to know where he was going, what he was up to.

So while everyone lined up for the cafeteria, I headed toward the bathroom, and when nobody was looking, I did exactly what Kevon had just done. I slipped away. But unlike Kevon, I didn't look as guilty.

By the time I got outside, I was way behind Kevon, who was walking fast. I wished my legs were as long as his because I could hardly keep up. At the same time, I wanted to stay far enough behind him to make sure he didn't see me.

Kevon didn't stop at any stores or anything. He just walked and walked and walked, for maybe thirty blocks or something. He had me zigzagging, taking shortcuts, going through alleys. Wherever he was headed, he knew where he was going. And he was gonna get there no matter how far away it was.

We went to a part of Newark I'd never even seen before. The neighborhood looked kinda bad, worse than where I lived, and the stores and apartments and everything were older and more run-down. When Kevon got to a corner and waited for the light to change, he started looking around. Real fast, I ducked behind a car. I didn't follow him all this way to get caught now. I had to be careful.

We walked two more blocks, and this time I stayed across the street, right near all the parked cars so he couldn't see me. This was a time when being short paid off.

Finally, Kevon stopped in front of a store called Paco's Bodega, but he didn't go in. He opened this door right next to the store with a key and went inside. I stood across the street and looked up. There were apartments over the store. That was probably where Kevon had lived before they took him away.

I stayed hidden for about three or four minutes, and that's when Kevon came back outside, looking half mad and half worried about something. When he went into the store, I took a chance. I crossed the street and got as close to the store as I could. I slid up to the wall outside the store, right by the big window, and heard Kevon talking to somebody.

". . . see him, Paco?"

I heard a man say, "No. Not after the night those people came and got you."

"He took off somewhere," Kevon said, sounding way more desperate than I'd ever heard him. "I need to talk to him. If you see him, can you text me? I'll give you the number."

That didn't make sense. How could anyone text him if there were no minutes on his phone?

"Alright," the man said.

"Thank you," Kevon said, "I gotta go now. Look out for him, okay?"

I guessed Kevon was heading for the door that was about two feet away from me. I had nowhere to go. I was about to get busted.

So I did the only thing I could think of. I turned around and bent down like I was tying the laces on my sneakers, and I got lucky because Kevon just walked right past me.

I waited till he got about a half a block ahead of me to start following him again. Was he going somewhere else now?

After a long time though, I realized he wasn't. He was headed back to the Center.

My spying mission was a success. I had learned something about him. Kevon didn't know where his father was, and he was worried about him. Everything he'd told the caseworker was a lie. His father wasn't working construction in Detroit. His father was missing.

TWENTY-THREE

THE NEXT MORNING, WHILE ME AND KEVON WERE eating breakfast, Mom sat down at the table and said, "Jarrett, I'm missing twenty dollars from my purse. Did you see it?"

I shook my head. "Me? No." Was she accusing me of stealing or something?

"Kevon?" she asked.

He looked up from his bowl of Honey Nut Cheerios. "Huh? Twenty dollars? No, I didn't see it." Then he put his head back down and kept eating.

Mom stared at both of us for a few more seconds and said, "I'm going to ask you both one more time, and I hope you're not lying to me." I could tell she was trying to keep her voice calm because Kevon was a foster child. If it were just me there, she wouldn't have been asking all nice like that. "This is not the kind of home we have here, where we take things from one another without asking. Did either of you take twenty dollars from my purse?"

Both of us said no. I knew *I* didn't take it, that was for sure. There was only one other person who could have done it, and he was sitting next to me drinking the rest of the Honey Nut milk from the bottom of the bowl.

▪ ▪ ▪

That day, we had the second and last day of shooting the trailer, and I had even more fun than I'd had on Tuesday.

The best thing about that day was the girls. Even when I was finished shooting the part with Caprice and Nicole, when they could have gone inside the Center to watch the basketball players, the girls stayed outside and watched me instead. That was the first time anything like that had ever happened to me, that was for sure.

"Okay, everyone," I screamed over all the talking and everything. "We're done. It's a wrap!"

Everyone clapped and I took a bow. I'm not sure why, but it just felt like the right thing to do.

It took me and Ennis and Lawrence a while to get all the props and equipment and everything back inside the building. "We're going to edit the trailer next week," Lawrence said. "So get ready for some hard work."

"I'm ready," I said. I liked editing even though it took forever sometimes. Funny thing was, my mind could always stay focused when I was editing videos. "Can we start now?"

"No, we're having a staff meeting in a half hour."

"Alright." I didn't like having to stop something right when I was in the middle of it. But I had to wait.

▪ ▪ ▪

The basketball team was still practicing, so I went to the gym to watch. I was planning to go sit with Caprice, maybe, but of course she was sitting with a whole bunch of girls. No way could I go up to her with all of them around her. It was impossible. So I sat in the front, near José and Yu. The two of them were always together now. "Y'all acting like real brothers," I told them, sitting down next to Yu.

"We *are* brothers," he said.

And José reached over and grabbed Yu around the neck and started fake punching him in the head. "See. Brothers," he said.

"I don't think brothers are supposed to attack each other," I said.

"That's 'cause you don't have a brother."

"What about Kevon? Isn't he your brother?" Yu asked.

"Nah, we're just like, I don't know."

"If you had a brother," José said, finally letting Yu go, "you would know about being attacked. My big brother used to beat me up all the time."

"What happened?"

"Jail," he said. "He stole a car."

"Dumb," I said.

"*Very* dumb."

We watched the guys play for a while. They were good, and even though I would never tell Kevon, he was one of the best.

It took me about ten or fifteen minutes before I noticed that Kevon's backpack was on the floor, right next to me. For the second time in two days, the spy part of me took over my brain, and I did what I'd done the day before. I bent down to tie my laces, which were already tied, and slipped my hand into that side pocket of his backpack, where he kept the phone. Real fast, I snatched it and stuffed it into my sock. "I gotta go to the bathroom," I told Yu. "Be right back."

I left the gym as fast as I could without letting the phone fall outta my sock. Nobody was in the bathroom, which was perfect. I went into the stall, pulled out the phone, and turned it on. This time, when I checked the minutes, it said:

500 Minutes/Unlimited Text

I checked the messages, but there weren't any.

Probably his father was still missing.

Meanwhile, I now knew for sure Kevon had bought a card to put more minutes on his phone.

He had stolen my mom's money. This was proof.

TWENTY-FOUR

AS SOON AS I GOT TO THE CENTER THE NEXT DAY, I went to find Ennis. I wished we could start editing the trailer, but Lawrence didn't work on Fridays, so post-production would have to wait till Tuesday. I would only have two days to edit with Lawrence, and even though I was trying to be cool about it, I couldn't help getting a little nervous that it wouldn't be done on time. Or that it would be done, but none of the kids would like it.

The only thing me and Ennis could do to work on the movie without Lawrence was listen to a bunch of music and sound effects he left for us, so we could choose which ones we wanted in the trailer and where. I don't know where he got them from, but they were real creepy and scary.

When Ennis clicked on the fourteenth track, both of us actually jumped back, then we laughed. It was a sound effect of what brains probably sound like when they gush outta somebody's head. "That's the best one," Ennis said. "But it doesn't fit our movie. We have to do a zombie movie next. A real movie."

He was back to that again.

I clicked on the next track fast, just to get him off that subject. We still had to find the right sounds for every little scene of the trailer, and we didn't have time to get distracted.

Me and Ennis worked for about an hour, till Miss Lisa came and got us for lunch. I sat with Ennis and a couple guys from the step team, but Kevon, also known as The Thief, sat on the other side of the cafeteria with the guys from the basketball team. They were all wearing their uniforms, and they were laughing loud and joking around. I don't know why it bothered me that he was on the team, but it did. That afternoon they were gonna be playing against some other Center from the South Ward, the first game with The Thief on the team.

Of course all the girls were sitting at the table right next to them, looking at them and giggling, which wasn't anything new, but it still bugged me. After the girls saw our step team in action, maybe they would be sitting next to us. That was what I was hoping for anyway.

"I gotta go," Ennis said after practically inhaling his hamburger and onion rings. "I told Mrs. Prajapati I was gonna teach the little kids to paint again."

"You like doing that?"

"Yeah. It's cool."

A little while after he left, the basketball team left, too, all at the same time. Their game was gonna start soon, and everyone was gonna be there to make sure they won. I really didn't wanna go, but there wasn't anything else to do. Ennis was busy, and all the other guys who weren't on the team were gonna be watching.

The only good thing about having to sit and watch The Thief play was that the bleachers on our side were kinda crowded, and there weren't a whole lot of empty spaces. But one of them was right next to Caprice, who was sitting with Nicole and all those girls. I hoped it didn't look too weird when I sat right next to her.

"Jarrett," she said, smiling. "See, I saved you a seat."

"No, you didn't," I said.

"Okay, that's true, but I'm glad you're here."

She was glad I was there. What was I supposed to make of that? Did she like me? What else could that mean? Was I supposed to say something back?

My brain was almost about to self-destruct. Then I heard someone on our side of the bleachers yell, "Get the ball, Kevon!" and when I looked at the court, The Thief had the ball and he made a basket that got everybody cheering. Then he pointed at a couple girls in the crowd, like he'd made the basket just for them or something.

It was almost too much to have to sit through. Except I was sitting next to Caprice, so I reminded myself to deal with it.

Only, the next time The Thief hit a three-pointer, and while everybody was cheering and chanting "Kevon, Kevon, Kevon," he actually pointed to Nicole and then — I couldn't believe it — to Caprice. *My* Caprice. The girl he knew I loved. And I had to sit there while her and Nicole giggled like The Thief was some famous basketball player or something.

Now *that* was too much. It was one thing to steal money from my mother who didn't even have a lot of money. But this was worse. He had crossed the line and broken the bro code. A guy is *never* supposed to go after somebody else's girl.

"Your cousin is so good," Caprice said, still smiling. She didn't even take her eyes off him when she talked. Those eyes followed his every move.

Without even thinking, I said, "He's not my cousin. He's nothing to me."

That got Caprice's attention. "What do you mean? I thought —"

"He's just some kid. I don't even know him."

I must have been talking loud or something because this guy Dontrae, who was sitting right in front of me, turned around.

"Who is he, then?" Caprice asked.

Dontrae nodded like he wanted to know, too.

Now I spoke louder, so that everyone around me could hear, even all those kids clapping and cheering for Kevon, a kid they only knew for a couple weeks. "He's a foster kid, alright?" I said. "He comes from some messed-up family with no mother and a crazy father. They had to take him and his little sister away from his dad, and now they have to live with us."

For about three and a half seconds, I felt good telling everybody the truth. I mean, it was about time they knew. I shouldn't have even started lying for Kevon in the first place.

But, like I said, that feeling didn't last long, just till I saw the look on Caprice's face, the way she was looking at me. It's hard to describe it, really. She looked like a mixture of shocked, sad, and mad — at me.

I saw some of the boys laugh, but not Dontrae. All he said was, "That's cold, Jarrett."

Caprice covered her mouth with her hand and whispered, "Oh, poor Kevon."

Poor *Kevon*? Why was he poor Kevon when I was the one who had to put up with that big show-off, sleeping in my room, stealing from my mother? Why did she look like she felt sorry for him, not me?

That was when she shook her head and said, "How could you do that, Jarrett?"

"What? I just wanted you to know he wasn't really my cousin, that's all."

"Then why didn't you just say that? Why did you have to put his business out there for everyone to hear?" She looked back at the court with those sad eyes. "That was wrong, Jarrett."

Then she stood up, passed by me, and climbed down the bleachers like she couldn't stand being next to me. Nicole shot me a mean look, too, even though it was hard for her to look mean wearing all pink and a glittery headband with little hearts on it.

I sat there by myself for a few minutes, not sure what to do. Caprice hated me, and for what? For telling the truth?

I told myself that none of this was my fault, not really. Kevon was the one showing off and pointing to the girl he knew I liked.

Whatever happened, he deserved it.

TWENTY-FIVE

I LEFT THE CENTER BEFORE THE END OF THE GAME and walked home by myself the way I used to all the time before Kevon invaded my life. When I got home, Mom was in the living room doing a giant floor puzzle with Treasure, Hugo, and Rafa. "Come help us," she said to me.

"In a little while," I told her, and went straight to my room, which was actually empty for a change. I didn't feel like climbing up the ladder, so I took off my sneakers and laid down on the bottom bunk, a bed that was still mine no matter who slept in it.

Caprice hated me. I hated myself. And none of this would have happened if it hadn't been for Kevon scoring that three-pointer, then trying to score a three-pointer with my girl.

Blaming Kevon wasn't gonna change anything with Caprice though. I had to figure out a way to fix things with her, at least get her to be my friend again. But after the way she'd looked at me, I didn't know if there was anything I could do.

I knew it wasn't gonna take long for Kevon to get back. The game would be over soon, and he was gonna find out what I'd told everybody. And he was gonna be mad.

There wasn't anything I could do anymore. So I laid there, waiting for him. And I got ready for what was about to happen.

About a half hour later, I heard the front door open and slam shut. Then, three seconds later, he was in my room. I jumped up off the bed, and me and him were standing there face-to-face for a long time. We were just looking at each other, mad, waiting for the other one to make the first move.

Kevon spoke first. Through his teeth he said, "I'm gonna kill you."

"Oh, yeah?" I wasn't about to back down. "Why don't you try?"

He pushed me on the shoulder, so I pushed him back. Then he pushed me again, and I pushed him again.

Then he pushed into me real hard, and I almost fell back. Before I could get my balance, he charged and knocked me down on the floor, right against my totem pole, which fell over and cracked at the top.

Now I was mad.

I was just about to retaliate when, next thing I knew, Kevon was on top of me and he was swinging at my head hard, so hard it took me a while to even know what was going on. "I hate you," he kept saying. "*I hate you.*"

He was hitting me so hard, but no way was I gonna cry or let him know he was hurting me. I couldn't do that, not in front of him. If I let him beat me up in my own house, I would never stop feeling like a loser.

So I used all the strength I had to get out from under him, which wasn't easy with him hitting me the way he was. When

I was far enough away from him, I swung my foot and kicked him right in the stomach.

Even though I wasn't wearing any sneakers or anything, I could hear the wind leave his body as he doubled over and hit the floor. It was my chance to get the advantage over him. So what if he was older and taller and bigger and all that? He needed to feel some pain, too.

I jumped up while he was still holding his stomach and I kicked him on the leg, then jumped on top of him and punched him on the side of his face. "I hate you, too," I said. "Just leave already. I hate you."

That was when I felt someone pulling my arm, then grabbing me on the shoulder. It was my mom, trying to pull me off Kevon, her precious foster kid. "Jarrett, stop!" she yelled. "Stop!"

But I was too pumped up to stop. "I hate him."

"He kicked me in the stomach!" Kevon yelled, getting up off the floor.

"He punched me, like, a million times!"

"I saved your life, stupid!"

"If it wasn't for me, you would be living on the streets, stupid!"

Mom stepped in between me and him. "What is the matter with you two? What's this all about?" She looked at me, then Kevon, then me again, like it was *my* fault or something.

I stood there breathing hard. How was it right that I could get attacked right in my own room?

"Talk to me!" Mom screamed.

Me and Kevon looked at each other. I wanted to know if he was gonna tell her that I told everybody the truth about him. Because if he did, I would tell her all about him sneaking away from the Center and stealing her money. If I was gonna go down, I was gonna take him with me.

But before either one of us could say anything, the babies ran into the room and all three of them were crying loud.

"See what you did," Mom said to me and Kevon. She wasn't screaming at us anymore, but it was close. "You scared them."

Hugo ran over to me and wrapped his arms around my leg, wiping his eyes on my jeans. Then Treasure threw herself down on the floor, still crying like she was losing her mind. Rafa just stood there with tears and boogers running down his face. He looked like he didn't know what was going on.

Mom picked Treasure up off the floor. "It's okay, baby. Your brother and Jarrett were just playing around. They're not fighting."

"Sure, lie to the kid," I mumbled.

"Shut up," Kevon said back.

"Hugo, Rafa, come on. Let's go back and finish the puzzle. Jarrett, come with me."

"Why do I have to leave my own —"

"Come!"

I stood there, glaring at Kevon for another couple seconds, but Mom wasn't going anywhere till I left, so I had no choice but to leave him there. None of this was fair.

Mom made me sit in the living room so she could keep an

eye on me. She might as well have put me in one of the baby cribs if she wanted to keep me a prisoner. I had nothing to do except watch her get the babies to stop crying and then get them to finish doing the big, stupid puzzle.

Finally, Terrence came by after work. Right away he was like, "Come on, everyone. I'm taking y'all out to eat. That General Tso's chicken with fried rice is waiting for me!" Terrence only looked that happy on paydays.

Mom got up to give him a kiss, but I just sat there with my arms folded.

"What's up, man?" Terrence asked me. "You looking like somebody stole your puppy."

"I don't have a puppy," I mumbled. "I don't even have a room anymore."

Terrence looked over at my mom, then back to me. "Trouble in paradise?"

"They were fighting," Mom said, talking about me like I wasn't even sitting right there.

"Fighting? Like, *fighting*?"

Mom nodded. "You wouldn't believe it, Terrence. I don't know what's wrong with them."

Terrence came over to the couch and sat down next to me. "What's going on?"

"My mother brought some kid into my house, and he attacked me. What else do you wanna know?"

I shot Mom a mean look, but she wasn't looking at me. She was back on the floor with the three babies.

"You wanna tell me what's up?" Terrence asked.

"Nothing," I said.

"What y'all fighting about?"

"Nothing."

"You wanna go to the Chinese Buffet?"

"I'm not going anywhere with him."

"And I'm not going anywhere with him." I looked up and Kevon was right there.

Terrence stood up. "Alright. We need to calm everything down with you two. Jarrett, come with me to get some Chinese takeout."

I looked over at Mom to see if she would let me go. When she didn't say no, I headed to my room to get my sneakers. When I passed Kevon in the hall, we just eyed each other but didn't say anything.

I went back to the scene of the crime and sat on the bottom bunk bed and put my sneakers on. When I stood back up, Kevon was standing there over me.

"What?" I asked.

"Nothing," he said.

Me and him were face-to-face again, about three inches away from each other. "You better not tell my mom what I did," I said.

"Or what?" He was acting all tough.

"Or I'll tell her you stole her money."

"I didn't."

"I know you did," I said. "And I know you snuck away from the Center, too." For a second, his face looked surprised, but then he tried to play it off. I thought about telling him I knew about the phone, just so he would know I'd found out what he was hiding, but I stopped myself. I needed that phone. I needed to know what he was gonna do with it now that he put minutes on it.

So we stood there for another couple of seconds, neither one of us saying anything. But we didn't need to. I could see on his face that we understood each other.

He wasn't gonna tell my mom what I did to him at the Center.

And I wouldn't say anything about her foster son being a sneaky, lying thief.

TWENTY-SIX

ME AND KEVON DIDN'T FIGHT AGAIN THAT NIGHT, but every time I looked at him, it just made me mad all over again. And not just at him. At my mom, too. Why did she think it was okay for me to have to live with a guy who tried to kill me in my own room? What did I do to deserve that kinda life?

It was like she was deliberately torturing me.

After me and Terrence came back with the Chinese food, Mom made me and Kevon sit at the table and eat together because that's what "civilized people do" or something. Like Kevon was a civilized person. Then she actually wouldn't let me throw Kevon outta my room. She was like, "The agency won't like it if I make one of my foster kids sleep on the couch." So guess who ended up sleeping there?

I wish I had an agency to look out for me.

▪ ▪ ▪

It was a good thing Kevon had basketball practice all day Saturday, so I didn't have to look at his stupid face. When he got back, he passed out asleep again, so I had time to get the place ready for Ennis.

Mom and Terrence left early for their date, and were gone by the time Ennis got there. Aunt Inez was cooking and the babies were running around. I wanted to talk to Ennis, tell him what happened, get him to see what kinda life I was living now that Kevon was there, but of course, it was hard to talk with wild animals running back and forth from the living room to the kitchen, screaming for no reason.

So I waited. Me and Ennis watched our trailer about a hundred times on Terrence's laptop. The editing still wasn't done, and we needed to put in the titles and the credits, but I could already tell it was gonna be good. And scary. Caprice was definitely gonna want a strong guy like me sitting next to her when she saw it, just so I could protect her.

"We need a name for our production company," Ennis said. "For the credits."

"Yeah!" My mind started racing. "Zombie Boys Productions."

"Monster Guys Productions," Ennis said.

"J&E Productions."

"I think you mean E&J Productions."

We both started laughing. "How about we do something with our names," I said. "Like, Jarris or —"

"What about Knight Crawford Productions?"

"Crawford Knight." I nodded. "Or CrawKnight."

"It should be Crow," Ennis said. "Night Crow. That sounds scary."

"Yeah," I said, even though his name was first. "NightCrow. Write that down. Fast."

"Jarrett!" Aunt Inez called me from the kitchen.

I got up and went in there. The food she was making smelled good, but still I wished she would have just let us get pizza or something the way we always do when Ennis stays over. Nobody wanted to eat real food on the weekend.

"Go wake Kevon up," she said, "and you kids come in here and get something to eat."

"Do I have to?"

"Go." She pointed down the hall.

I looked over her shoulder to see what she'd made. Some kinda chicken, and a big pot of peas and rice. And she had some codfish soaking in a bowl of water on the counter next to the stove for breakfast tomorrow.

I slowly walked down the hall to get Kevon, trying to figure out a way to tell him to come for dinner without actually *talking* to him. But before I got to the door, Treasure and Hugo ran down the hall, so I got an idea. "Hugo," I said, "go tell Kevon 'come eat dinner.'" I said it three times to make sure he got it.

I opened the door and stood there and listened as Hugo told Kevon to come eat dinner. And yes, he said it three times. Kevon got up and passed me on his way to the kitchen. I didn't have to say anything to him.

Babies *were* good for something.

▪ ▪ ▪

After dinner, Kevon went to give Treasure her bath. I told Ennis to pick out a movie for us to watch, and while everybody was busy doing something, I slipped into my room and checked Kevon's phone as fast as I could. But there was nothing. No calls, no texts.

"What's up with you and Kevon?" Ennis asked me when I got back to the living room. "You didn't say a word to him all night."

Aunt Inez was still in the kitchen with Hugo, so I had to whisper. I told Ennis about everything that happened the night before, and how much I hated Kevon.

"I don't even get why you were fighting," Ennis said.

"Kevon was showing off for Caprice!" Why was this so hard for him to understand?

"If Caprice likes him, there's nothing you can do about it. And you won't even tell her you like her."

"He knows I like her. He should back off. That's the bro code. When *you* like a girl, would you want some other guy showing off for her?"

Ennis shrugged. "I don't like a girl."

"But when you do, you're not gonna want —"

"Look," Ennis said. "I don't like girls, and I don't think I ever will. Okay?"

"But . . ." What he said surprised me, and I didn't know what to think. Or say. So I just looked at him. His face was more serious than it had ever been. Then I remembered Man Group and that question someone had asked Terrence. It had to have been Ennis.

When I didn't say anything right away, Ennis said again, "Okay?"

I nodded. "Yeah. Um, yeah. It's okay."

"Good then," Ennis said. And we just looked at each other for about five seconds.

He was the same old Ennis. Nothing was different. And nothing was gonna be different, not with me and him. I knew that for a fact.

Ennis reached for the remote control. "Ready for the movie?"

"Yeah," I said, laying down on my sleeping bag. "You pick. But make it a good one with lots of guts."

TWENTY-SEVEN

YOGA WAS GETTING HARDER. AND SO WERE MY toenails. They were like a bird's talons now. And they were sharp like bone. I could hear them scratching against the yoga mat whenever I had to get into a different pose. I knew everyone could hear them, and it was embarrassing.

I had to quit yoga.

"We're all getting better," Caprice said to me after class was over.

"You're talking to me again?" I couldn't believe it, not after the way she looked at me on Friday.

"Yeah, I still think what you did was wrong, but this class, you know, yoga, it makes me want to forgive you. Let things go."

"Thanks," I said. I liked that she wasn't still mad at me. "Yoga is good for that kinda stuff."

"I know. I wish we could have this class every day."

"That's what I was thinking." Okay, maybe I had gone too far, but I liked talking to her, even if it was just about yoga, and I didn't want our conversation to end.

"Caprice?" I started.

"Yeah?"

"I, uh, have to tell you something." I looked around the room, just to make sure nobody was listening to me because I was thinking about going for it. We were standing so close together, and we were both kinda sweaty, but she looked really beautiful sweaty.

"Is it about the movie trailer?" she asked. "I can't wait to see the whole thing."

She was making me feel more pressure to make the trailer good, but that wasn't her fault.

"I told my mom and dad about it," she said, "and they're gonna come and see it on Monday."

"Good. Good." This was so bad.

"What did you want to ask me, Jarrett?"

"I, uh, I wanted to know if you . . . if you wanted to be in my next trailer."

"Yeah! Of course! What's it about?"

"I didn't write it yet, but I got lots of ideas, I mean, now that I know you're gonna be my star."

Caprice couldn't have been more happy, and like most directors, I got all the credit. She put her arms around me and gave me a quick — way *too* quick — hug. But it was something.

Kevon had to go home early because his caseworker was coming to see him and Treasure again. Me and him still weren't talking, and I didn't wanna go home with him, but I knew my mom would have a fit if we didn't come home together. Anyway, I wanted to use that opportunity to spy on him and his caseworker again, so I didn't mind going home earlier than usual.

The caseworker came around 6:00, right when Mom was feeding Treasure and Hugo in the kitchen. I think Treasure was getting into Guyanese food because she kept stealing the plantains from Hugo, and all he did was say, "No. Bad girl. Mine."

Treasure laughed in his face. Then she poked him in the arm, and he poked her back. I had no idea what they were doing.

The caseworker looked in on Treasure and checked her forehead. "That's healing nicely," she said to my mom.

"Yes, it is. I hope it doesn't leave a scar."

They talked for a little while, and I stood in the living room trying to figure out how I was gonna do my spying this time. I could have hid in the closet again, but it was hard to hear anything that way. I could try hiding in the living room, like, maybe behind the couch. But there wasn't any room for me, not with all the toys and stuff back there.

I looked around and that was when I got the best idea. It was too good to be true.

Right there, right on top of one of the little play tables in the corner, was Terrence's laptop. Before I could talk myself outta it or tell myself it was too risky (or just too wrong), I ran over to the computer, opened it real fast, and pressed the button for the video cam.

Of course that stupid green light came on, and right then, at the same exact moment, I heard Mom say, "Why don't you and Kevon go into the living room so you can talk in private?"

My hand reached up to close the laptop, but then I had another, even *more* genius idea. Instead of closing it and messing up my chances to find out what I needed to know, I spun the laptop around so the screen and that stupid green light faced the wall. I wouldn't get to see what they were doing, but I would still get to hear everything, and that was more important.

When the caseworker and Kevon walked into the living room, I walked out real cool, so they wouldn't know I was up to something. In the hall, my mom eyed me like I was doing something wrong.

"What?" I asked.

She kept staring. "I hope you're not up to something."

"Like what?"

More staring.

"Can I go to my room?" I asked.

"Go on," she said.

I went back to my room and closed the door. I had to wait and hope nobody found out that laptop was secretly recording them.

■ ■ ■

Later, after the caseworker left, I knew Kevon was depressed because when Mom told him Treasure needed her bath, he said, "It's okay. You can do it."

Me and Mom looked at each other, like we couldn't believe what we were hearing. Something must have happened to him if he was actually gonna let my mom take care of Treasure. That just made me wanna hear what had happened in that living room even more.

Mom told him okay, and then she made me and Kevon go into the kitchen to eat. Together.

I didn't get a chance to grab the laptop, but I played it cool while I ate. I needed to finish fast though, so I could get to the laptop first, just in case Kevon decided he wanted to use it or something.

I could hear my mom in the bathroom with the babies. She'd probably put them in the tub together because they were laughing their brains out in there. But in the kitchen, it was quiet. Kevon looked like he was stuck in his own head.

"You okay?" I asked him after a while, even though I still wasn't talking to him. For some reason, I thought I could get some answers outta him, especially when he was so miserable.

But he just shrugged.

"Did your caseworker say when you can go back home?"

"No."

"Oh." I wanted more information, but I knew he wouldn't tell me anything. I needed to get to that computer.

A little while later, Treasure and Hugo ran down the hall in their pajamas, screaming. First they came into the kitchen, and then they went into the living room.

I kept eating. Fast.

When the babies didn't run outta the living room, I got a bad feeling. They were up to something in there.

Kevon got up and put his plate in the sink. I wasn't sure if he was gonna go in the living room, but I had to make sure he didn't see that laptop. I jumped up as fast as I could, practically dropped my plate in the sink on top of Kevon's, and ran to the living room.

And that's when I saw them. The babies. They were standing right in front of the laptop, looking at themselves on the screen, bouncing their heads back and forth as the video cam recorded them.

I wanted to scream, "No!" but I couldn't because Kevon came into the living room right behind me and I didn't want him to see. So I stood behind the kids, blocking Kevon's view, and closed the laptop real fast.

Of course Treasure started crying and then so did Hugo. "No, *Jawett,*" he screamed. "No."

"It's not yours," I said. "You can't play with Terrence's laptop. You're gonna break it."

From her room, my mom yelled out, "What are you doing to those babies, Jarrett?"

"Nothing. They were playing with the laptop."

Treasure wrapped her arms around my leg. I wanted to pick her up, but I didn't want to leave the laptop on the table and risk Kevon picking it up. So I came up with another brilliant plan.

"You guys wanna watch some videos?"

Hugo nodded, and then so did Treasure.

"Okay, sit down and I'll find something good."

A few minutes later, they were watching funny kid videos on the laptop, and I didn't have to worry about Kevon getting his hands on it. As a matter of fact, he got so bored after ten minutes, he just went to my room.

When Mom came and got the babies for bed, that was my chance. I looked around real fast, just to make sure I was alone. Then I grabbed the laptop and flew into the bathroom at top speed. Fast but quiet.

I locked the bathroom door, ran the water in the sink loud, sat on the toilet seat cover, and listened to the recording of the secret meeting between Kevon and his caseworker.

TWENTY-EIGHT

ABOUT FIFTEEN, TWENTY MINUTES LATER, I TURNED the water off, closed the laptop, and quietly opened the bathroom door, sticking my head out very spy-like. The coast was clear. I had to get this laptop back to the living room before Mom found out it was missing, because she would know that I was up to something. She was good that way.

I ran down the hall, slipped the laptop back on the table where I found it, and got back to my room in less than twenty seconds. Kevon was already asleep, which was good because I didn't even know what to say to him now.

I climbed up on my bed and laid there with my eyes closed. I needed to think.

The truth is, my brain was spilling over, like lava coming outta a volcano, all because of what I'd heard on that laptop. In my head, I couldn't stop the words from replaying over and over. It was like a movie script or something. One of those really, *really* sad movies my mom likes to watch.

CASEWORKER: I went by your apartment on Friday.

KEVON: Why? I already told you my father is in Detroit, right?

CASEWORKER: Nobody was at your apartment, so I talked to some of your neighbors in the building and —

KEVON: What are you talking to them for? They don't even know —

CASEWORKER: Two of your neighbors, they told me they saw you there last week, that you stopped by and they thought you were looking for your father.

KEVON: (angry) They're lying!

CASEWORKER: *Both* of them?

(Silence)

CASEWORKER: Kevon? You have to talk to me. Why would you be there looking for your father if he's in Detroit working on a construction site? And why hasn't your father come back home when he's been unable to contact you? Wouldn't he be worried about you and Treasure?

(Silence)

CASEWORKER: You're not telling me something, Kevon. I'm trying to help you, but if you don't tell me what's going on, I can't. You have to be honest with me.

KEVON: (quieter) I am.

CASEWORKER: Where is your father now? Did he hurt Treasure? Are you trying to protect him?

And that's when I heard it. At first, I thought it was Treasure from the other room, but no. It was Kevon. He was crying. Crying like a little baby, right there in front of the caseworker. And she was telling him the kinda things adults tell kids, like, everything is gonna be okay and he was in a good foster home, and all that. But he just cried and cried.

And in the middle of all that crying, he said, "I wanna go home. I want my dad."

I shouldn't have heard that. But I did. I mean, I already knew Kevon was lying about where his father was. But now I got it. No matter how he acted all the time, like he was a man or something, Kevon was just a kid who wanted his dad. That was it.

As I laid there on my bunk bed, thinking, I wondered why I never felt the way Kevon felt. Why didn't I ever want my father? Why didn't I ever even really think about him?

Maybe I was missing something. I wasn't sure.

▪ ▪ ▪

The next night, while Kevon was giving Treasure her bath, I decided to check his phone again, just to see if there were any messages. The phone wasn't in that same side pocket this time. He had it inside his backpack, underneath his basketball uniform, so I knew he'd definitely used it since the day before.

I turned the power on, and when I checked for messages, this time there were three of them, probably from that guy who owned the store:

ur dad is back. call the store kevon.

call me. ur dad want to see u.

ur dad is doing bad kevon. call the store he
want to see u and baby.

The messages all had different dates on them, but Kevon hadn't answered any of them. That was weird. I knew for a fact Kevon was trying to find his father. The day before, he was crying for him. But now that his father was back, Kevon wasn't even doing anything to see him.

I put my finger on the Reply button, but I didn't know what I would say. If Kevon's father wanted to see him, maybe I should tell him where Kevon was living. Maybe his father would come and take them back home with him. Wasn't that what Kevon wanted?

I clicked on the Reply button, but before I could think of what to write, Treasure ran into my room at top speed completely naked, laughing and laughing like she had just done the funniest thing in the world.

"Treasure!" Kevon called from the bathroom.

As fast as I could, I powered off the phone and slipped it back into Kevon's backpack. Less than a half second later, Kevon ran into the room holding a towel. "Treasure, what's the matter with you?"

He moved closer to her, but she ran away again, this time

over to me. I caught her, and Kevon came over and wrapped her little naked body in the big towel.

My heart was still pounding. Loud. I'd almost been busted with that phone.

As Kevon dried Treasure off, all she did was laugh. When she first got here, all she did was cry all the time. But those past few days, she definitely laughed more than cried. She was changing. She was happy here.

TWENTY-NINE

KEVON HAD TO STAY AT THE CENTER FOR PRACTICE the next day, so I walked home by myself. When I got there, I could tell from my mom's face that something was wrong. She was in the kitchen feeding Hugo and Treasure, and when I came in, she looked at me and pointed to the stack of mail on the other end of the table. "It's the letter."

"What let — ?"

"From Central Boys Academy."

My breathing stopped. "It came?"

She nodded. And the look on her face told me everything I needed to know.

I failed.

I'd have to do sixth grade over again.

Mom handed me the letter, but I didn't need to read it.

"We'll talk about this later, Jarrett," Mom said, getting up from the table. "The caseworker is coming for Hugo in a little while." She picked up Hugo from his chair and then Treasure from her high chair. Both babies ran outta the kitchen. "Slow down!" Mom ran after them, leaving me standing there, still holding the letter in my hand.

I don't know what I wanted her to do or say to me, but it felt like she just ignored me, like getting that letter wasn't the worst thing in the world to me.

I sat down and put the letter back on the table. Everything I did, all the work I did all summer was for nothing. Mrs. Greer knew I was gonna fail and she won.

I sat there at the kitchen table for a long time, just thinking about what this whole thing meant for me, for my whole life. I would always be behind everybody else. Everyone would know how dumb I was. Nothing would ever be the same again.

I was still in my head when I heard the caseworker come. Her and Mom were talking in the hall, just the usual stuff, when Mom asked the caseworker, "Where is he going?"

"His grandmother is going to take him," the caseworker answered.

I didn't know what was happening inside me, but before I could think about it, I jumped up and ran outta the kitchen. "What?" I practically yelled. "Why would you let his — ?"

"Jarrett?" Mom's voice was sharp and angry. "This doesn't have anything to do with you."

"Yes, it does!" I was screaming now, not so much at my mom as at the caseworker. "I saw what his mother did to him, and how do you know his grandmother isn't gonna let his mother get to him?"

"His mother is in jail," she said to me. "She can't hurt —"

"Well, what if she gets outta jail, like, on bail or something?"

"Hugo's grandmother is a good woman. We checked her out very carefully. She's going to protect him. Don't worry, okay?"

"Don't worry?" What was wrong with that lady? How could I not worry about Hugo, the happiest kid I ever met. A kid with a big iron burn on his chest. How could I stop worrying about him?

I saw my mom hand Hugo over to the caseworker, and I couldn't take it anymore. I couldn't stand there and watch her take a picture of him and say good-bye when I'd never get to see him again. It wasn't right and it wasn't fair. I couldn't even look at Hugo and watch him leave and not know if he was gonna be okay where he was going.

So I ran down the hall to my room and slammed the door behind me.

It hurt. Everything hurt, like inside my chest and stomach. I couldn't breathe, but it wasn't like I was having an asthma attack again. I was feeling something and it hurt. I just didn't know what was more painful, failing summer school or losing Hugo.

I couldn't take this anymore.

It took a long time, but finally Mom came into my room. I was on the top bunk, so she stood next to the bed and grabbed my hand. But it was too late as far as I was concerned.

I pulled my hand away. "Forget it," I said, not looking at her.

"Jarrett, I know you're upset, but that doesn't give you the right to be rude, especially to me. I didn't do anything to —"

"You're right. You didn't do anything. All this time, for, like, the last two or three years, you never did anything to help me. You knew I was behind everybody else. You knew I couldn't really read that good, but all you cared about were the babies. Not me. *Them*."

I heard Mom take a deep breath. "I know you're looking for someone to blame, but —"

"Forget it," I said again. My heart was beating really fast and really hard. "You don't have to be in here."

"C'mon, Jarrett," Mom said. "You can't let yourself get this upset. I don't want you to have another asthma attack."

I wanted to say something, but I was too mad to talk anymore. Too full of feelings. I pushed my face into the pillow because I thought I was gonna cry, and I wanted to stop it before it happened.

Anyway, right then, at that same exact second, Treasure ran into the room, and my mom went back to ignoring me. "I know you miss Hugo, right, sweetheart?" I heard her say. "I know, baby. It's hard."

And then Treasure started crying, and even though I didn't want to admit it to myself, I knew how she felt.

Mom put her hand on my back and told me to try to rest. Then I heard her leave my room with Treasure.

That was all the time I got.

■ ■ ■

That night, I heard Mom and Terrence having another one of their non-fights. It wasn't loud and I probably wouldn't even have heard them if I had been able to fall asleep. But I was wide awake thinking, which was even more depressing since I had to listen to Kevon sleeping like he didn't have anything to worry about at all.

Just like before, Mom and Terrence were fighting about going away somewhere. But this time Terrence had a real plan. He wanted her to go away with him on Friday. "My friend's cabin is free all weekend," he said. "It's the last weekend of the summer. We can bring the kids with us."

"I can't just take foster kids away on a trip. The agency —"

"Call them in the morning," he said.

"Terrence, I'm so tired of you telling me what to do."

"I want to take you away on a trip. Why you gotta — ?"

"I'm saying, it's not that easy."

"It could be if you wanted it to be."

Back and forth. Back and forth. If their arguments were in a movie, it would be the boring part where you get up to go get popcorn or go to the bathroom or something.

I laid there, listening, not sure which way I wanted it to end. I wouldn't have minded getting away from around here and sleeping in a real cabin somewhere. Just as long as we were back in time for the Labor Day block party on Monday. At the same time, spending two or three days stuck in a cabin with Kevon didn't really sound like any kinda vacation to me.

Anyway, there wasn't anything I could do about it. Nobody was asking me if I wanted to go or not. Just like everything else in my life, I had no control.

THIRTY

THE NEXT DAY WAS THE LAST ONE ME AND ENNIS would get to work on the movie trailer with Lawrence. And there was so much left to do.

But we had step practice first. I tried to shake off my bad mood and get into the step routine, but I still wasn't good at it. It was like I just couldn't remember the order of the steps or something. Maybe all those teachers were right about me. I couldn't learn anything.

If I didn't wanna look like a fool in front of Caprice, I would have to practice this weekend.

Lunch was fun though, and it took my mind off everything else. Not only was everybody talking about our trip to Six Flags Great Adventure the next day and what rides they were gonna go on and everything, but the Center made these nasty hard Tater Tots and everybody started chucking them at each other across the cafeteria. Two of them hit me right in the face, and those things hurt, too. But I knew who threw them — Dontrae — so I got back at him. A lot of mine missed him though, but Yu was there keeping my supply of ammunition steady.

Then Miss Lisa came out from the kitchen and saw what we were doing, and she started yelling at us for wasting food. "Don't you know about all those poor starving kids in Africa?"

"Even starving kids can't eat rocks!" José yelled back, and everybody laughed.

"That's it," Miss Lisa said. "Lunch is over. You kids don't even deserve to get free lunch if this is the way you're going to behave. C'mon, bring your trays up."

Everybody groaned. We still had twenty minutes left for lunch, and she was messing up all the fun.

On my way back to the video room, Caprice came up to me and whispered, "Are you okay?"

"Yeah, why?"

"I heard about, you know, school." She was still whispering. "Don't feel bad about it, okay, Jarrett?"

My feet and my heart both stopped. I looked at her face hard. "Huh?"

"I know about you getting held back, and I just wanted to say it's okay. It's not such a big deal, so don't worry —"

"How did you even — who told you?"

"Kevon. He just wanted to —"

"He *told* you?" I really couldn't believe what I was hearing. What kinda guy was he? Why would he go up to Caprice and tell her something like that?

And how had he found out anyway? I hadn't said a word to him last night. He must have seen the letter from Central Boys, the one I'd left on the kitchen table like a big idiot.

But I didn't have time to think about that. I looked away from Caprice and scanned the hall for Kevon. It took me a while to find him, but there he was, all the way at the other end.

I flew down the hall, and when I was close enough, I pushed him as hard as I could. "Why you had to violate me like that?" I yelled.

Kevon pushed me back. "Don't mess with me, little boy."

"Why you had to say anything?"

"I thought she already knew, stupid."

By that time, me and him had a crowd around us. They looked like they were ready for a fight, and so was I. I was tired of him, tired of having to put up with somebody who couldn't even keep his mouth closed about stuff that wasn't even his business.

I pushed him again. "You the one that's stupid," I said. "You the one crying the other day like a baby." I looked around the room. "Y'all should have seen that, the way he was crying to his caseworker. You wouldn't believe it."

Kevon balled up his fists and I knew he was gonna punch me, but I didn't care. I was ready for him this time. But before he could hit me, Dontrae came outta nowhere and grabbed him. All he kept saying was, "Come on, man. Come on. You don't need to do this."

And Ennis was by my side telling me the same thing. "Come on, Jarrett. You don't wanna get in trouble."

I even heard Yu say, "You don't need to fight, Jarrett. Walk away."

Easy for him to say. He didn't even come to the Center every day. He didn't have to deal with these kids all the time. If I walked away from this fight, I would have everybody thinking I was some kinda punk, and they would never let me forget it.

When they pulled us apart, I saw Mrs. Prajapati standing there with her arms crossed and the maddest look I ever saw on her face. "What is going on here?" she asked.

I was still staring at Kevon, too mad to say anything.

"Mr. Crawford. Mr. Underwood. Is this how you young men conduct yourselves? And you're family, too."

Both of us said at the same time, "He ain't my family!"

"Either way, you boys live together and you should have more respect for each other. And for this Center. Look at all the younger kids here watching you. Is this the kind of role models you want to be?"

She was trying to make us feel guilty, but it wasn't working on me. She didn't even know why we were fighting. If she did, she would understand why I had to kill him.

"Tomorrow is the big trip," she said, and even before she finished, I knew what she was gonna say. I could feel it. "You boys are no longer invited. I can't risk having you two fighting on the bus. I'll be calling your mother today."

Then she told the staff to keep an eye on us for the rest of the day so there weren't anymore "troubling incidents."

When she walked away, Kevon said, "Good thing she came before I —"

"Before you what?" Now I was mad all over again and the crowd got back around us, waiting.

But Ennis was right there. He grabbed me away and put his hands on my back and pushed me down the hall, away from everybody. He pushed me into the art room and closed the door behind us. Nobody was in there, which was good because I had a lot to say and most of it wasn't the kinda thing a guy should say in front of girls.

I couldn't believe Kevon. After everything me and my mom had done for him, he still had the nerve to open his mouth about my private business to everybody.

"He was just getting you back," Ennis said, like I needed to hear that.

"Getting me back for what? For letting him sleep in my room for, like, a month? For letting him eat my food and breathe my air?"

"For telling everyone he's a foster kid and that his father is crazy."

"He *is* a foster kid and his father *is* crazy!" Ennis was really making me mad, too. "You don't know anything, Ennis. So stay outta it."

Ennis shrugged, all calm and annoying. "You're losing your mind, Jarrett."

I didn't even wanna go back out there with everyone, now that they all knew I couldn't make it outta sixth grade, even after going to summer school. What was I supposed to say to them? And Caprice? No matter what she said, I knew she would never let me be her boyfriend now. She was smart and did good in school. Why would she wanna be with a guy like me?

Ennis sat there drawing on a big piece of cardboard while I stood there being mad. Actually, I couldn't stand still. I needed to walk back and forth being mad. It took me a long time to calm down, and all the time Ennis just sat there drawing, not even helping me stay mad at all.

Eventually, me and Ennis went back to the video room to work with Lawrence, and we had so much work to do, I actually stopped thinking about how much I hated Kevon. That's what I like about editing. It takes your mind off everything else.

"You guys did a great job," Lawrence told us when we were done. "I can't wait to see everyone's face when you show it on Monday."

"Think they're gonna be scared?" I asked, because if they weren't, there wasn't any point in showing it.

Lawrence laughed. "Definitely."

I smiled. "Good."

When we left the video room, most of the kids were in the gym watching the basketball game against some center in Paterson. The last thing I wanted was to watch Kevon play ball, but I had a plan.

I went to the gym and I sat there watching the game for a while, playing it cool, even after some of the guys said stuff to me like, "Man, how dumb do you have to be to fail sixth grade *and* summer school?" And "Dumb is cool now, Jarrett. You alright."

Thanks, I wanted to say. *What a nice thing to say to a guy.*

I would be hearing stuff like that for my whole life now. I knew it. I had to find a way to deal with it.

But I didn't let it distract me from my plan.

While everybody was focused on the game, I jumped down below the bleachers and crawled on the floor over by where Kevon had his backpack. I knew what I needed to get. And this was the perfect opportunity.

I didn't even need to move his backpack. I just reached my hand through the seats and into that side pocket where he kept the phone. In a second I had it in my hand, and I was crawling back under the bleachers and straight out the door. When I got in the hall, I didn't know where to go, especially with that phone in my hand, so I stuck it in my pocket and ducked into the boys' bathroom. I went into a stall, turned the phone on, and looked at the messages. Kevon still hadn't texted the store owner back about his father.

So I did what he wouldn't do. I hit reply and wrote back:

> tell my dad I need him to come & get me NOW.
> im waiting for him. come right now.

I added the address to the Center so Kevon's father would know where to go. Then I hit Send right away and stood there waiting to see if he would text me back. But after ten minutes, nothing. I deleted all the old messages so Kevon wouldn't know what I did. Then I turned the phone off again, stuck it back in my pocket, and did everything I did before in reverse. By the time I put the phone back and got back up on the bleachers, the only one that even knew I was gone was Ennis. He asked me where I'd gone and I said the bathroom.

It wasn't a lie.

For the rest of the game, I kept looking around the gym, waiting to see when Kevon's father was gonna get there. Where *was* he?

When the game was almost over, Terrence came to the Center. "Your mother didn't want you two walking home by yourself," he told me, sitting down next to me in the bleachers. "Especially not after what happened here today."

"She mad?" I asked, knowing the answer already.

"What you think?"

I sat there, shaking my head. It wasn't even my fault. What other choice did I have after Kevon did something like that to me?

"We going up to my buddy's cabin in the morning," Terrence said, "if the agency lets your mom take the kids. Might as well leave early since y'all can't go on your trip anymore. Maybe some fresh air will get you boys thinking straight."

"I doubt it," I said.

Then I thought maybe I could find a way to get Kevon lost in the woods forever. I tried to hide my smile, just thinking about it.

THIRTY-ONE

I WOKE UP IN THE MORNING ALREADY MAD. I couldn't believe I wasn't going on the trip to Six Flags with everybody else and now, just to make my life even worse than it already was, I had to spend the next three days in a stupid cabin with my enemy.

After I got dressed and came out to the kitchen for some food, I overheard Mom on the phone, probably talking to Kevon and Treasure's caseworker. First, she gave the caseworker the information on where we were gonna be over the weekend, and even gave her Terrence's phone number in case she couldn't get any service on her own phone.

Then I heard her say the thing I'd been dreading the most. She said, "School starts on Wednesday, and I need to know if I should register Kevon at a school near us. My son is going to be starting at Central Boys Academy. I can see if there's room for Kevon there. If not, there's another school right in the same building."

In my head, I screamed, *Noooooo!* But in real life, I just stood there, frozen, breathing hard, head spinning. *This can't be happening,* I told myself. *He was only supposed to be here for two or three days.*

I couldn't think of what would be worse — him going to Central Boys, a school I didn't even wanna go to, or him being in the school downstairs, my *real* school, the one with all my friends.

Treasure came running outta the living room and ran up to me with her arms in the air. I picked her up. "What are you doing?" I asked her. "Waiting for Mom to get off the phone?"

I carried her back to the living room and put her down on the floor. I would've gotten dragged into playing with some dolls if my mom didn't call out, "Jarrett, Treasure, come and eat breakfast! Terrence is gonna be here soon to pick us up."

Treasure had to be picked up again and carried into the kitchen. When we got there, Mom said, "And where is your brother?"

Those words almost made me drop Treasure. *My brother?*

Then I figured out she was talking to Treasure, not me.

▪ ▪ ▪

The only good thing about being stuck in the backseat of Terrence's car with Kevon was that we didn't have to sit next to each other. Treasure's car seat was in between us. Outta all of us, she was the only one having fun. She was listening to the music Terrence was playing and kicking her feet and clapping her hands.

"I wish Ennis could have come," I said, even though I knew there was no way he was gonna give up the trip to Six Flags just to come to some dumb, boring cabin.

"Next time," Mom said.

To get to the cabin, we had to drive to upstate New York, which took almost four hours because we had to stop twice — once so Mom could change Treasure and once because we were hungry. We were far away from the city, so far away all we saw were trees and cows and grass and nothing else. Then, finally, we pulled off the highway, to some small winding road that went around a lake.

"We're here," Terrence said, pulling up in front of this cabin that was kinda small and beat-up looking. "This is Fred's cabin."

Mom looked at the cabin and back at Terrence. "Are you sure?" All the cabins around that lake looked exactly the same.

"Yeah, this is it. We used to come up here for a week every summer and play poker all night. Back when we were young and could eat fried food for days at a time and didn't need things like sleep." He laughed as he hopped outta the car and went around to open the trunk.

I sat there for a few seconds. This cabin looked like the kinda place you see in those horror movies, where there's some crazy killer in a mask running around at night. As a matter of fact, I wished Ennis was there even more because it would have been the perfect location for our next trailer.

While Kevon got Treasure outta her car seat, I grabbed my duffel bag from the trunk. As I walked to the cabin, Mom came up behind me and slipped her arm around my shoulder. "I hope you're not planning to be this miserable all weekend."

I didn't say anything.

"Because you can decide to be happy if you want to be."

"Yeah, right."

Mom kissed me on the cheek. "Look around. Isn't it nice up here? Well, the cabin is on the creepy side, but the lake is beautiful, isn't it?"

I shrugged.

Mom added, "I just hope there aren't any big spiders or snakes in that cabin." Treasure ran up to us. "See, Treasure's happy to be out of Newark."

She was a baby. She didn't know any better.

"To tell you the truth, Jarrett, I wasn't really in the mood to come either, but Terrence was so excited to show us this cabin. Now that I'm here, I'm going to choose to have fun, no matter what the inside of that cabin looks like, and I hope you do, too."

She made it sound so easy.

■ ■ ■

An hour later, everybody was doing something except me. Terrence and Kevon were playing with a football, running around, throwing it back and forth. Mom and Treasure were playing in a little blow-up baby pool Terrence found in the garage.

Me, I had climbed the biggest tree I could find, and I sat there as long as I could, just watching them. I felt like one of those cameras that directors put up on a crane or something so they could let the audience see all the characters the way birds see them, small, like ants. I mean, I wasn't *that* high up, but at least I wasn't down there with them, acting like I was having fun when I wasn't.

I chose not to be happy. And I planned to keep choosing not to be happy as long as Kevon was living with us.

When it started getting dark, Terrence called up to me, "I need you and Kevon to go around to the side of the cabin and grab some of that firewood, in case the cabin gets cold tonight."

I looked down and shot my mom a look. "Do I have to?"

"Yeah," she said. She picked Treasure up outta the pool and wrapped a big towel around her. "Both of you boys. Work together."

They were so obvious. Adults always think kids don't have real reasons to be mad at each other, that if I carried some dumb wood with Kevon, I would forget how much I hated him. If they knew the truth about what kinda kid he was, they would know there was no way that was ever gonna happen.

I climbed down as slow as I could, and walked around to the side of the cabin where there was a pile of wood in this metal rack. Kevon got there first and grabbed two pieces. "That's all you're gonna carry?" I asked, even though I didn't wanna say anything to him.

"I only got two hands."

He was so annoying.

"And it's not even gonna get cold," he said.

"Why don't you just admit you're weak?" I loaded one of my arms with three pieces and then put two more in the other. They weren't even heavy. Kevon walked away and got around to the door before me. Then, instead of holding it so I could get in, he just let it slam closed, right in front of my face.

When I tried to balance the wood and open the door, three of the logs fell outta my hands and landed on the ground loud. From inside the cabin, I could hear Kevon cracking up. I stood there for a long time, trying to calm myself down, telling myself not to run in there and punch him.

Even if he was asking for it.

▪ ▪ ▪

For the rest of the night, I tried to stay away from Kevon as much as I could. I stayed outside with Terrence while he grilled hamburgers and hot dogs, and I ate next to Treasure at the picnic table, on the other side of the table from Kevon. And then when Mom and Terrence decided to take a walk by the lake at night, I stayed behind them. Kevon walked with Treasure, holding hands. Mom walked with Terrence, holding hands.

I was by myself.

When we got back to the cabin, Mom was like, "Okay, it's time for the kids to go to bed so the grown-ups can have alone time."

"That's not fair," I said. Why did they get to be alone, and I had to be stuck with Kevon?

"Do what your mother says," Terrence said. He was already in the kitchen opening a bottle of wine.

Me and Kevon went to what was supposed to be our room for the weekend. "So, which bed do you want?" he asked me.

The room had two beds that looked exactly the same. "Does it make a difference?"

"I'm just asking," he said. He threw his stuff down on the bed closest to the window, which, of course, was the one I wanted.

I sat on the other bed and kicked off my sneakers. The room was too small for two people. There wasn't enough space between the two beds. They were only like three feet apart. It was bad enough sleeping on the bunk bed on top of him, but now I would have to actually *see* him.

THIRTY-TWO

THE NEXT MORNING, TERRENCE WOKE ME AND Kevon up real early. "What's wrong?" I said, still half asleep.

"We're going fishing," he said, standing over my bed.

I turned over, away from him. "I'm tired."

"C'mon, man. We got to get out there to that lake before all them other families get all the fish."

"That doesn't make any sense," I mumbled.

Then Kevon said, "I never went fishing before." I heard him get outta his bed. "I'm gonna be ready in ten minutes," he said.

"Nah," Terrence said. "Make that *fifteen* minutes. You gotta wash up better than that."

I flipped back over on my back, my face tight and mad. If Kevon was gonna go fishing in that dumb lake, I had to go, too.

■ ■ ■

It was my first time fishing, too, so the whole morning was like being in a different world. Terrence took us to some store to buy bait, and then we drove to what he called "a good spot" on the lake. We didn't have a boat, so we just walked out on some wooden dock and fished off the end.

Terrence was right about one thing. People came out real early to fish. By eight o'clock, there were a whole bunch of boats, and the dock was getting crowded, too.

"We don't have any food for dinner," Terrence told us. "So if we don't catch anything, we don't eat anything."

I sighed long and loud. Now it was *my* job to feed everybody. Like I didn't have enough to worry about already.

It took a long time for any of us to catch anything, even when we tried using different kinda bait. Terrence looked like he was having the best time of his life, and even Kevon was having fun not catching anything. But me, I still couldn't get into it.

Then I got a tug on my line.

"I feel something!" I shouted, and my heart started beating harder as I tried not to drop the fishing pole in the water.

Terrence ran over to me and put his hand over mine. "Keep steady," he said, and he showed me how to reel the fish in. When it came outta the water, flopping around like crazy, I couldn't help but laugh, especially since I was the first one to get a fish. Terrence helped me swing my pole over the railing and take the fish off the line.

After we dropped the fish in our bucket, I said, "That fish looks weird."

"It's a brown trout — a nice big one, too." He patted me on the back. "Good catch."

After that first fish, we spent about two more hours catching all kinds of ugly fish. By then, the pier was so packed with people, we decided to head back to the cabin. I couldn't wait to show Mom the ones I caught.

On the way back to the car, Kevon walked along the edge of the lake, jumping from big rocks to big logs like he was the only one who knew how to do that. I followed him, doing the same thing, and it wasn't even all that hard either.

"Don't bust your necks!" Terrence called out.

"I won't," I yelled back.

And right when I said that, it happened. Kevon's feet slipped on a log, and he went flying right into the edge of the lake — the muddiest part, too.

The first thing I wanted to do was laugh, but even in that split second, I knew what would happen if I did. Kevon would go back and tell my mom, and I would get in trouble.

But I didn't have to worry about that because Kevon started laughing first. He was lying there in the mud laughing, screaming, "It's freezing! Aargh, it's freezing!"

Terrence started laughing too. Then me. I couldn't help it. It was funny, so funny I wish I could have caught the whole thing on video. It was taking Kevon so long to get up, too, like he was stuck in quicksand or something.

"Help the man, Jarrett," Terrence said.

I had no choice. I went over to Kevon and reached out my hand, not sure if he was even gonna take it. But he did. I pulled him hard, but instead of him getting outta the mud, I ended up going in sideways. He was right, too. That mud was freezing! But that just made us laugh more.

"Y'all ain't getting in my car," Terrence said. "You know that, right?"

I didn't care. Once you're in the mud, there's nowhere to go but muddier. Before we knew what was happening, we were having an all-out mud fight, and I have to admit, it was kinda fun.

By the time we were finished, Terrence was gone, and me and Kevon looked like swamp monsters.

There was another dock not too far away, a small one that had steps going into the water. "Let's swim all this mud off us," I said.

"Can't," Kevon said. "I don't know how to swim."

"You never learned how to?"

He shook his head.

Weird. My mom signed me up for swimming lessons when I was about five or six. Some kid in Newark drowned at a pool, and she said she didn't want that to happen to me. I'm not the best swimmer in the world, but I'm not scared of the water the way I used to be when I was little.

"I'll teach you," I said.

Kevon looked terrified.

"I'm not gonna let you drown. Come on."

Us two mud creatures walked over to the dock, and after a lot of talking, trying to get Kevon to trust me, he climbed into the water after me. It wasn't all that deep, just like up to our necks, so we got the mud off, and then I tried to teach him how to float. He was definitely scared, but he tried. And for me, it felt good being better at something than Kevon for, like, the first time.

After a while we were both hungry, so we walked back to the cabin. It was hot and the sun was drying us off. "Don't tell anybody at the Center I fell in the mud," Kevon said.

"The way you didn't tell anybody I got held back?" I knew I shouldn't be bringing all that up after we were just kinda being friends, but I couldn't help it. I was still mad.

"The way you didn't tell anybody about my family. You started it, Jarrett. My family is *my* business."

"*You* started it when you showed off for Caprice. She's mine, you know."

"You're crazy. I'm not thinking about Caprice. I know she's yours."

"Good, then."

"Good."

We walked the rest of the way without talking. Dealing with him wasn't easy. I didn't hate him, but it was hard being friends with him. It was like we were in between.

The rest of the day was good though, and me and Kevon didn't even fight anymore. We ate lunch, played with Treasure, then did some more swimming lessons in the lake. Then, while we were drying out on lounge chairs, we started talking about the block party.

"I can't believe I'm gonna get to show my trailer in two days," I said.

"You been working on that a long time."

"Yeah. I just need to get through the step team routine first."

Kevon jumped up. "Well, you been teaching me how to swim, so I'll teach you the routine."

For the next hour and a half, all we did was practice over and over again till I got it, till I knew I wasn't going to embarrass myself in front of Caprice.

■ ■ ■

That night while everybody else was in the cabin, me and Terrence stayed outside grilling all those fish we caught.

"I need to talk to you about something, Jarrett," he said.

"Me?"

"Yeah." He looked around like he was checking for spies. "Me and your mom, we been going out for over a year, and you know how I feel about her, right?"

"Yeah, you love her, right?"

"You know it." He smiled. "So, I thought up here, by the lake, this would be the perfect spot to ask her if she wanted to marry me."

"Marry you?" My voice was way too loud.

"Shhh." Terrence laughed, looking around to make sure no one else had heard. "Yeah. But I wanted to ask you first, because I was hoping to get your permission."

"*My* permission?"

"Yeah, if she says yes, then that would mean you're getting a stepfather. You want me for your stepfather?"

I smiled big. "Yeah, of course."

Terrence dropped the big grill clippers he was holding and grabbed me in one of his man hugs. "To tell the truth," he said, "I already feel like your stepfather, kid."

The word *stepfather* sounded kinda strange to me, too close to the word *father*. It was something I needed to get used to.

He finally let me go. "Alright, just don't say anything to your mom. I wanna surprise her, okay?"

"I know. I'm not gonna say anything."

"Don't forget, Jarrett."

"I won't!"

Terrence didn't know who he was dealing with, a master spy who knew how to keep his mouth closed.

THIRTY-THREE

ON SUNDAY, WHEN I WOKE UP, I WAS ACTUALLY kinda excited. It was our last day at the cabin, and it was Treasure's birthday. But those weren't the only reasons. I was excited because I knew today was the day Terrence was gonna ask my mom to marry him.

It was a busy day. First, we all drove into the nearest town to buy a birthday cake for Treasure and some balloons and stuff. We weren't really gonna have a big party or anything, but Mom wanted to make sure she knew it was her special day. Then we came home and decorated the cabin.

Even though he was going through the motions of having fun, I could tell Kevon wasn't really into it. It was like his body was in the cabin, but his brain was somewhere else. After the cabin was looking kinda partyish, Mom came over and put her arms around Kevon and said, "Everything okay?"

He shrugged, "Yeah, why?"

"You look a little sad."

"No, I'm okay. I just don't get why you have to do all this just for a birthday. She's only two."

"Because every child should have a birthday party. Have you ever had one?"

"Yeah, when I was little. You know, before —" He shook his head. "Forget it."

I knew what he was gonna say. Before his mom died. But that didn't make sense for why he was upset now. He was probably acting this way because he still didn't know where his father was.

Maybe I should have told him about the messages, about how that guy from the store had seen his father. But then he would know what I'd done, that I stole his phone and tried to get his father to come to the Center. Then me and him would start fighting again.

"Can I go for a walk?" Kevon asked my mom.

"Okay," she said. "Don't go too far."

"And get attacked by a bear," I added.

A worried look crossed Mom's face. "Terrence, are there bears up here?"

He laughed. "He's gonna be okay, Kimma. Let the man take a walk."

When Kevon got back, we had Treasure's party. We sang "Happy Birthday" and ate cake with no ice cream. Then, even after everything was done, Treasure didn't wanna take off that party hat for anything. "She's probably gonna wanna sleep in that thing," I told Mom.

"I should have gotten her a plastic one that would last longer." Mom picked up Treasure. "Okay, pool time for the pretty party girl! Let's get your bathing suit on."

"C'mon, guys," Terrence said. "We gotta get the pool ready."

We went outside and got the hose out. I started filling up the little pool first, and I waited for Kevon to want a turn, but it didn't look like he cared. He was still in his mood. "Can I take another walk?" he asked Terrence.

"Nah, man. It's gonna get dark in a couple hours, and I don't need to have you out there by yourself."

"I'm not gonna get lost," Kevon said. "I'm not stupid."

Mom came outta the cabin with Treasure, and both of them were in their bathing suits. "Oh, good. Our pool is ready for us!"

As soon as Treasure got in the pool, she started splashing water on Mom. "Stop that, Treasure," Kevon said. The way he looked at her was weird, like he was real mad at her for acting like every other two-year-old.

"Don't worry about it," I said. "She's just having fun."

"It makes no sense."

"What's wrong with you anyway?"

"Nothing."

Terrence came up behind Kevon and put his arm around him. Then they walked away and I followed. "What's going on, man?" Terrence asked. "You got something on your mind? Talk to us, man to man to man."

Kevon pulled himself away from Terrence's arm and walked some more. Then, finally, he stopped and turned around. It took him a little while to talk, but we waited. Terrence taught us in Man Group that men got a lot of feelings, too. Not just girls. But sometimes us men needed more time to talk about ours.

Finally, Kevon said, "My mom. She died when . . . I mean, the day she died, that was the same day —" He stopped again and looked down at the ground.

"Go on, man," Terrence said.

"My mom. She was pregnant with Treasure, and she was coming home from work and she got hit by a car real bad. And when she got to the hospital, they said they couldn't save her, but . . ."

"But they could save Treasure?" I asked.

He nodded.

"That's so —" I couldn't think of what to say. It was like too much for my brain to process or something.

"I'm sorry about that, Kevon," Terrence said. "That's rough. Two years ago — that's not a lot of time to deal with something like that."

Kevon shook his head.

"You gonna be alright," Terrence said. "You and Treasure, y'all gonna be okay. Just stick together and look out for her."

"I know. That's what I do."

We stood there for a little while, and it was getting more and more sad because nobody said anything. Then Terrence put his arms around both of us. "I know what we need."

"What?" we both asked at the same time.

"War. Nice friendly war."

Kevon looked confused. "War?"

Terrence got a crooked smile on his face and nodded slowly. "War."

■ ■ ■

A couple hours later, all three of us limped outta Lakeside Paintball tired and in pain. I don't think there was one spot on my body that didn't ache. Paintballs hurt. A lot. As we got back in Terrence's car, he said, "I told you guys, war ain't no joke."

Me and Kevon just groaned.

Back at the cabin, Mom was lying on the couch, reading a book. "My men are back from the battlefield," she said. "Tell me all about it."

Terrence shot me a look, and I said, "Me and Kevon are tired, Mom. We're gonna go right to bed."

"But I'm hungry," Kevon said.

I was kinda hungry, too, so I said, "We're gonna eat real fast and then go to bed, okay, Terrence?"

"Cool," he said. "Fast!"

Mom sat up. "What's going on here?"

"Nothing," I said, and pushed Kevon into the kitchen.

"Ow," he said. "I'm a wounded man."

"If you were a man, you wouldn't complain."

Me and Kevon ate some more of the fish and corn Terrence made yesterday, and even ate another piece of Treasure's birthday cake. "Why are we rushing?" Kevon asked. "It's not even nine o'clock."

"Shhh," I whispered. "I'll tell you later."

I looked over at Mom and Terrence in the living room. He had his arm around her, and they were sitting all close together on the couch. If we hadn't been around, they would have probably been kissing or something. And then Terrence would probably ask her to marry him, and she would say yes, and then everyone would be happy.

Especially me.

■ ■ ■

In our room, it took us a long time to change into our pajamas, that's how much our bodies hurt. "Why did I let Terrence talk me into doing paintball?" I asked him.

"But that was fun though."

"Remember when that kid was hiding behind that big rock, and we ambushed him."

We laughed.

"Yeah," Kevon said, "but then his big brother got me right on my butt. Oh, man, that still hurts!" He put his hand on his butt and spun around in a circle, going, "Ow ow ow ow ow."

I laughed real loud. "Them kids probably been there a hundred times."

"I know. They were like a real military unit. And their dad was crazy."

"But Terrence got him good!"

I got up and turned the light out. Then we got on our beds, still talking about everything and laughing. Finally, Kevon said, "I'm gonna miss it up here."

"Me, too," I said. I hadn't even wanted to come here, and now I didn't wanna leave.

We didn't say anything for a while, and up there in the cabin it was so quiet. I never heard *nothing* like that in Newark. There was always something going on outside, no matter what time of night.

"Terrence is gonna ask my mom to marry him. That's why he wanted to get rid of us."

"You want that?"

"Yeah, why not?"

"Nothing. He's cool."

"I never had a stepfather before," I said. "Or a real father either."

Kevon didn't say anything.

"Do you miss your father?" I asked him. "I mean, I know you don't know where he is and —"

"You don't know anything about my father. You think you know, but —"

"Then tell me."

It took so long for Kevon to say anything back, I thought he was mad at me again for getting in his business. Or maybe he had fallen asleep. I wasn't sure, and the room was so dark, darker then it ever got in Newark with all the streetlights and car headlights and everything. In that room, the only light was from the moon coming in through the little window, and all I could see was the outline of Kevon's body, and he wasn't moving.

Then he said, "My dad is sick. Not sick sick but, like, his head is sick. And, no, he's not crazy like you told everybody at the Center. He just got problems. He used to be okay when my mom was here. He took his pills and everything, but now . . ."

"He stopped taking them?"

"Yeah. I always told him to take them, and sometimes I would break them up and put them in his food when he wasn't looking, but I think they stopped working because he got worse and worse. So I had to take care of Treasure all the time because he couldn't anymore."

"Did you tell anyone at school? Because I think somebody could have helped you if you —"

"I didn't tell anybody because I knew what was gonna happen. They were gonna take us away. If Treasure didn't get hurt, everything would still be fine."

"How did she get hurt? You never told me."

"You never asked."

"Well, I'm asking you now."

That was when Kevon told me it had been an accident, that nobody had hurt Treasure. He was giving her a bath, and she jumped up and hit her head on the faucet. "Blood was everywhere, Jarrett. It was gushing outta her head, and I couldn't think of any way to stop it. I thought she was gonna die, for real."

Kevon said his father was, like, frozen. Scared. Kevon had no choice except to call 911, just like he did when I was having my asthma attack. "But before the ambulance got there," he said, "my dad, he ran away. I don't know what happened. There was so much blood and maybe he thought they were gonna blame him, but he didn't do anything wrong. It was an accident."

"You think he's okay now?"

"I don't know. I'm trying to find him, get him back on his pills. Then he can come back and tell the caseworker he was in Detroit working and wasn't even there when Treasure got hurt. They'll have to let us go back and live with him."

Now I was the one who didn't say anything. I'd thought Kevon had a real tough life, but I hadn't known it was *that* bad. I shouldn't have been so mean to him. I should have tried to make everything easy for him, like be his friend instead of his enemy.

At the same time, if they let Kevon go back and live with his father, I didn't want him to take Treasure with him. Kevon could take care of himself okay. But Treasure, she was just a baby.

"This is all my fault," Kevon said. "I should have just watched Treasure better, you know?"

"Babies always jump around, Kevon. That's what they do. And I should know. I've had babies living with me my whole life. Like, thousands of them."

Kevon laughed. "Thousands?"

"A lot!"

I know I should have probably told him about the texts right then. But I couldn't. If I told Kevon what I did, all it would do is make him mad at me all over again.

So instead we went to sleep.

THIRTY-FOUR

IN THE MIDDLE OF THE NIGHT, IT HAPPENED AGAIN. I didn't know if it was because it was so quiet outside or if Terrence's voice was just louder than normal, but it sounded like he was really mad. "What's wrong with you?" he said. "Why won't you let anybody love you?"

I sat up in bed and listened, ready to go out there and protect my mom if I needed to.

"Calm down," Mom said. "The kids are sleeping."

"I want you to focus on *me* right now," Terrence said. "Not the kids. Me."

"I am. You know I love you. Why do we have to —"

"Because that's what people in love do, Kimma. They get married and stay together. Why is that so hard to understand?"

I couldn't hear what Mom said, but I heard what Terrence said next loud and clear. He said, "I don't know what that guy Grantley did to you, but you don't know how to let another man —"

"Leave him out of this, Terrence. It has nothing to do with him and you know it."

Grantley. I knew that name. I saw it on my birth certificate. *Grantley Crawford*.

My father.

"What's the matter?" It was Kevon, sounding like he was more asleep than awake.

"Nothing."

"They fighting again?"

"No. Just talking loud."

"I thought he was gonna ask her to marry him."

So did I. My head was spinning with questions. What happened? Why didn't Mom just say yes, she would marry him? Did this mean Mom and Terrence weren't going to be together anymore?

"Who are they talking about?" Kevon asked me. Even though the room was totally dark, I could see that he was sitting up, too.

Now I was the one who needed a long time to say anything because I think I had a lot of feelings, too. I wasn't sure if I should tell Kevon anything, but he did tell me a lot of stuff that night. "My father," I said.

"You got a father?"

"Yeah, but not really. I never met him or anything. But he's somewhere, I think." I was just rambling now. "I mean, I don't care where he is."

When I was little, I used to ask my mom about my father, and where he was, and all she ever said was he was her boyfriend in college, but he wasn't ready to be a father. So she left college early and raised me by herself. With Aunt Inez helping her. She made it sound like she never even thought about him again.

"You never wanna meet him?"

"No." I shrugged. "I don't know. I don't even know anything about him."

I thought about what Terrence said, that Grantley did something to my mother. "I don't think he's a good guy. I think he was mean to my mom or something."

I stopped talking again. It wasn't till I said that out loud that I knew why I never asked my mom about him. Because I didn't wanna know.

But still, even after the argument stopped, and me and Kevon had laid back down, I couldn't stop thinking about it. About him. My father.

Where was he anyway? And why didn't he ever wanna see me?

Kevon and Ennis talked about their fathers all the time. And here I was with a father somewhere. A father who knew he didn't want me even before he ever met me.

THIRTY-FIVE

THE NEXT DAY, MONDAY, WE PACKED UP THE CAR and drove back to Newark. It was Labor Day, the day the Center was throwing the big block party, and I couldn't wait to get there.

Mom and Terrence hardly talked the whole way home, and when they did, it was obvious they weren't the same anymore. I didn't know what happened, but I knew for a fact I wasn't gonna get Terrence as my stepfather.

It was a good thing me and Kevon were talking again, because the whole ride home would have been dead quiet otherwise. He was talking about a slam-dunk contest they were gonna have that afternoon, outside on the basketball court. And I was talking about the fact that the trailer was finally gonna premiere after the block party was over and everyone was back in the Center for the Kids Night open house.

Terrence pulled up in front of our house, and Mom got out without even giving him a kiss the way she always did when she got outta the car. I looked over at Terrence real fast to see if he was upset, but he was just looking at Mom like he didn't know what went wrong either. Yesterday, he thought he was gonna be getting married, and now he couldn't even get Mom to talk to him.

After Terrence was gone and we were upstairs, Mom grabbed the stroller and said, "You boys get ready for the block party. Treasure and I are going to pick up some snacks for Kids Night and drop them off at the Center. We'll be right back."

When they were gone, me and Kevon got dressed real fast. Qasim told all us guys to wear white T-shirts so when we did our step routine we would all look the same. Me and Kevon put grease in our hair and extra musk oil, just so we looked and smelled as good as we could. It was already almost 1:00 and the block party was probably already going on.

"Let's practice one more time," I said. I knew the steps now, but I needed to practice looking smooth.

Instead of one time, we practiced five or six times, till I was positive I could do it. Then Mom came back and she looked weird. Kinda scared almost. She came through the door and locked it right away.

"What's the matter?" Kevon asked her.

She shook her head. "Oh, nothing. It's just that there was a homeless man out in front of the Center, and when he saw me, he tried to follow me inside. But some guys there blocked the doors and gave me time to leave through the side door. I think Treasure got scared though. She started crying."

"Did he follow you here or something?" I asked.

"No, I don't think so. The poor guy just needed help." Mom picked up Treasure. "Let me change her, and then we have to get over there. It's already getting crowded. Kevon, don't forget your basketball uniform."

"Oh, man, I almost forgot." He ran back into our room.

I stood there, starting to get excited. Between the step routine and then the big premiere of the movie trailer, I could feel this was gonna be a good day. Probably my last good day before school started on Wednesday, when I would be the dumb kid in sixth grade. Again.

■ ■ ■

Just like Mom said, the block was packed by the time we got there. There was so much going on, I didn't know where to start. Kevon went over to the guys from the basketball team, and I walked around looking for Ennis. I found him sitting at a table, drawing on a big sheet of paper.

"What's going on?" I asked him.

"I'm drawing caricatures for a dollar each."

He was smart. Sitting in front of him was one of the old men from the seniors program. When I looked at the picture Ennis was drawing, he made the man's ears look four times the size they really were. Yeah, the man had big ears, but Ennis made them look kinda like Dumbo ears or something.

I started laughing. Ennis was such a good artist. No way was I gonna let him draw me. He would probably make me, like, two feet tall.

I stood around talking to Ennis for a little while till he was done with the picture. Then, instead of a dollar, the man gave him *five* dollars. So me and Ennis headed over toward the food tables.

On the way, we got close to where Caprice and some of the girls were having a double dutch contest. I wanted to stop and say hi to her, but there weren't any guys over there, and I didn't want everybody knowing I liked Caprice. So I kept walking.

There were a lot of games going on everywhere, especially stuff for the little kids. Everybody was running around, music was playing loud, and the food smelled so good. Me and Ennis ordered some barbecue wings and sat on the curb to eat them. Then I heard "Don't eat too much" and then there was that familiar laugh.

I looked up. "Terrence. I didn't know —"

"How am I gonna miss this block party? And your step?"

"Shhh." I looked around. "It's a surprise."

Terrence laughed again and held up his hands. "Okay, alright."

"What's a surprise, Jarrett?" That voice, coming from behind me, belonged to Caprice.

It took me a few seconds to turn around, not till after Ennis elbowed me. I jumped up and faced her. "Um, nothing. Just something I'm doing, um, for my . . ."

If I wasn't looking at her, I might have been able to lie better, but she looked even prettier than usual. Shorts, red T-shirt with *Jersey Girl* on the front, and her hair was down, not in a ponytail the way she usually had it.

I had to tell her how I felt about her. I had to.

"For who?" she asked.

"For my, um, my little foster sister, Treasure. She just turned two yesterday."

Caprice smiled so big, and for half a second I felt like a hero, till I remembered I didn't really have a surprise for Treasure. "I better get back to the double dutch contest," she said. "I can't wait to see the trailer tonight." She waved at me and took off down the block.

All I could do was stand there and watch her.

"So, that's the girl, huh?" Terrence asked. I'd forgotten he was standing there.

I nodded.

"You tell her you like her yet?"

I shook my head.

"I keep telling him to," Ennis said, which was just what I needed, both of them ganging up on me, pressuring me.

"C'mon, man," Terrence said. "You gotta take a chance."

I couldn't help but say, "The way you took a chance and asked Mom to marry you?"

"Man," Terrence said, and I could tell he was hurting. "Your mom, she's hard to love, you know. She keeps me away, like, arm's length."

I thought I knew what he meant, but I wasn't sure.

"She got a lot of hurt inside her," he said.

"But do you still love her?"

"Yeah, I do. I love her. But sometimes, I'm not sure if that's enough, you know?"

Now I felt like the one with a lot of hurt inside him. "Am I still gonna see you? Are you still gonna —"

"No matter what happens between me and your mom, I'm not going anywhere, you hear me? And I'm still gonna come around for Man Group." He put his hand on top of my head, which was weird, and pulled me into a real hug. Even though I knew everybody could probably see us, I hugged him right back.

▪ ▪ ▪

An hour later, Terrence was helping out with the water balloon fight, Mom was with Treasure and a whole bunch of three- and four-year-olds drawing with chalk on the sidewalk, and I was standing over by the DJ with Qasim and half of the guys from the step team, waiting for our music to come on so we could start our routine. Across the street, Kevon and the rest of the guys were waiting, too, trying to act cool, like we weren't up to anything.

Then the song came on, and I got so excited, I could feel myself kinda bouncing up and down. Qasim had to put his hand on my shoulder and say, "Remember, Jarrett. You gotta be cool."

I nodded. "Gotcha. Cool."

Dontrae and José got things started by stepping from the curb out to the middle of the street. It took a while till people started noticing, till I could see heads turning in our direction. Then the rest of us stepped out there, till we were all in the middle. The music stopped and Dontrae shouted, "One! Two! Y'all know what to do!"

The music came back on, and we went into our routine, and the crowd went crazy. I can't even tell you how good it felt hearing all the girls screaming and cheering for us. None of us missed a step, and none of us lost our cool.

We were smooth.

And when we were done, we stood there in our final pose and just let everybody clap for us. We all looked like we were Kings of Newark. My eyes, of course, were busy searching through the crowd for Caprice, and when I found her, she was giggling like crazy. I think that's what I liked about her the most, how happy she was all the time. It was hard not smiling, too, but I couldn't. I had to stay cool.

"You did it, man," Kevon said afterward, coming up behind me and patting me on the back.

"I never could have if you didn't —"

"Forget about it," he said.

Then we walked over to Mom, who clapped again when we got closer. "That was fantastic, boys!" She put her arms around both of us and gave us both a kiss on the forehead, me first.

That's when Treasure started crying. She had stopped drawing on the sidewalk with the bigger kids, and now she was looking down the street crying.

I looked over and saw who she was looking at. It was a man with a big, bushy beard. Even though it was real hot, he was wearing this dirty army jacket. But that wasn't the thing that made me and everybody else notice him. No, it was the look in his eyes. He looked like he was in a trance or something, like in one of those zombie movies.

"Oh, no," Kevon whispered. "No."

The man was still staring right at Treasure, getting closer and closer to her. Then he held his arms out like he was gonna pick her up, but Mom was on it. Fast. She grabbed Treasure and held her close.

"That was the man, Jarrett," Mom whispered. "The one who was following us."

Then, outta nowhere I heard Kevon say, "Why are you — what are you doing here?"

The man looked up, and when he saw Kevon, he looked like he was seeing a ghost. His mouth opened, and it took him a while to say something. Then he said what I had a bad feeling he was gonna say: "I'm here, Kevon. I got the message. Come back home. You can come back home now."

Kevon pushed me as he tried to move away from the man, his father. But by then there were so many people crowded around us, trying to see what was going on, Kevon couldn't really go that far.

His father started yelling, "I want my kids! Gimme my kids! I want my kids!"

A couple of girls started screaming and running away.

Then I heard a kid say, "Yo, that's Kevon's father."

And someone else said, "He looks crazy."

Then a woman said, "Shhh, don't talk like that."

It didn't matter. Kevon just stared at his father with a face that was mad, worried, and embarrassed, all at the same time. I didn't know what I would have done if I was him and that was my father. I probably would have run away and never come back.

Two seconds later, Terrence put his arms around Mom and Treasure, protecting them. He walked them across the street, while some of the other men on the block surrounded Kevon's dad, who was still screaming, "You can't steal my kids! Gimme back my kids!"

Finally, two police officers came from the other end of the block. They moved Kevon's father away from everybody and talked to him for a little while, but they didn't arrest him. They just walked him to the corner and made him leave the block party. Then they stood there for a long time, making sure he didn't come back.

After what Kevon had told me about his father, I felt bad for the man. It looked like he didn't even know what he was doing, like he really missed his kids and thought somebody had kidnapped them. Mom was right. He definitely needed help.

And I was the one who had brought Kevon's father back. That meant I was the one who had scared Mom and Treasure, and embarrassed Kevon in front of everyone at the block party.

It was all me.

THIRTY-SIX

I DIDN'T KNOW HOW, BUT AFTER A WHILE THE block party picked back up and everybody started having fun again. Not us though. Mom was sitting on the curb with Treasure, who had finally calmed down, and I was standing over them, trying not to talk to Kevon because I didn't know what to say to him. I was happy when some of the guys from the basketball team came to get him. They were like, "We gotta put on our uniforms for the slam-dunk competition."

"I'm not feeling it anymore," Kevon said.

"C'mon, man," one guy said. "Just forget about what happened."

How was he supposed to forget about his own father?

"Go on," Mom told him. "Try to have fun. Treasure's okay now."

The slam-dunk contest was a lot of fun to watch, except for when Kevon got up. Even though he was a good basketball player, you wouldn't know it by how he was playing that day. Every time he got a chance to show off his skills, he made one mistake after another.

At first everybody was clapping for him, trying to make

him feel better, but after a while, I heard some kids booing him. Good thing the other guys on the team were a lot better than Kevon. They were doing all kinda moves, showing off for the crowd. By the end, when it was Kevon's last turn, he just passed the ball to the next guy. He gave up.

"That was embarrassing," Ennis whispered as we walked away.

"Yeah, I know. I feel bad for him."

We had to go into the Center to help get everything ready for the premiere of our trailer. Inside, Lawrence was already there setting up the big screen and the projector. "Y'all ready?" he asked us.

"Yeah," I said. "Can't wait."

Ennis wanted to see it one more time, so we stood there watching it on Lawrence's laptop, which had the final version on it, the one with all the titles and sound effects and everything. It was perfect, too.

The whole gym was set up for the Kids Night open house. On one side of the room there was artwork everywhere, and on the other side, there was a little stage area with a huge screen behind it.

I had to be patient. Before we got to show our trailer, we had to wait for all the parents to see the artwork, then sit through all the kids' dances and karate demonstrations. Then Lawrence was gonna show a video he took of us all summer so the parents could see everything we did and all the fun we had.

Then, after all that, it would be showtime for *Terror in the Hood.*

So I waited while all the parents and kids looked at the artwork. My mom was talking to another lady with a baby in a stroller, and Treasure and the other kid were holding hands the whole time.

Terrence was there, too. He wasn't standing with Mom, but at least he didn't leave. He was laughing with some of the guys from Man Group.

It took a while till some kids came over to sit. I looked out as the bleachers started to get crowded, searching for Caprice, but she wasn't there yet. Kevon was sitting all the way on the top row by himself with his head down. He was probably still upset and embarrassed. It took me a while to see that he was looking down at something, but I couldn't see what he was doing.

While the dancing and everything else was going on, me and Ennis stood on the side of the bleachers. I didn't know about him, but I was way too nervous and excited to sit down. I didn't think my heart would go back to beating normal till after it was all over.

When the dancing and karate were done, Lawrence signaled for the lights to go down. Then he showed the video he made. Every time one of the guys saw themselves on the screen, they were like "That's me" or "Yo!" As for the girls, all I heard were little squeals and giggles when they saw themselves.

When the video was done, the kids and adults clapped for so long, till Mrs. Prajapati came out to the mic to thank Lawrence for working so hard with the kids.

Me and Ennis went over to the laptop to get our video ready to go. I looked out into the audience, and Caprice was in the second row sitting next to Nicole. Her mom and dad were there, too, sitting right behind her.

Lawrence stepped up to the mic and said, "Okay, our final video of the night is something I worked on with two of our aspiring filmmakers, Jarrett Crawford and Ennis Knight. These two young men wrote, produced, directed, and edited this movie trailer by themselves. They put in a lot of hard work and they were very dedicated to making this something special for you all. So sit back and prepare to be scared."

Everybody clapped and laughed, but I was only watching Caprice. I knew right after the trailer was done and everybody saw how talented we were, that was when I was gonna do it, tell her I liked her and ask her to be my girlfriend.

Lawrence gave the signal to the guy on the other side of the room who was in charge of turning the lights down, and as they were going down, Kevon came running down the bleacher steps. I was too busy getting ready to start the trailer, so I didn't really have time to think about what he was doing. Was he really leaving *now*, right before it started?

But he wasn't leaving. He was heading right toward me and he was waving something in his hand, but it was too dark to see what it was. It wasn't till he got close enough to me that I could make it out:

His phone.

"*You* did it!" he screamed at me, loud enough for everybody around us to hear. "You told him where I was! You told him!" He was close enough to me now that I could see his eyes and how mad he was.

"Wha-what are you talking about?" I asked, stepping back.

Ennis stepped in between us and said, "Kevon, stop."

But Kevon pushed Ennis outta the way and came back at me again. He got right in my face. "You sent a text to Paco, the guy that owns the store downstairs from where I live. It's right here." He pushed me, and I hit the table with the laptop on it, but it didn't fall.

"You're crazy," I said.

Kevon pushed the phone in my face. "See right here." On the phone it said *Sent Messages*. "This is your text."

"How do you know I wrote that?"

"Because I know you. I knew you were up to something."

That's when Lawrence yelled out, "Can someone put the lights on!"

A second later, the lights were back on, and now everybody in the whole audience could see me and Kevon standing there, him staring me down like he wanted to kill me. But I wasn't gonna back down, not with everybody watching. Not with Caprice sitting about two feet away. "I didn't do anything," I said, "so get outta my face."

He balled up his fist and I knew he was gonna hit me, but Lawrence and Ennis were there, and before anything could happen, they separated us. A lot of the kids on the bleachers were saying stuff like "Fight, fight" and "Get him, Jarrett." But Lawrence had pulled me so far away from Kevon, there was no way we could fight.

Not that I didn't wanna hurt him. I tried to break away from Lawrence, but before I could, Kevon looked me in the eye and knocked the open laptop off the table. Then, while it was on the floor, he stomped on it over and over and over. "Stop!" I screamed, pulling myself away from Lawrence.

But before I could reach Kevon, he kicked the broken laptop and shouted, "Now try to show your stupid movie." Then he walked outta the gym.

I stood there, looking down at the laptop, the only one with my movie trailer on it. I felt like crying — that's how mad I was. My trailer was ruined and I was standing in front of a whole audience, so embarrassed, so mad, so —

I couldn't even think straight.

Things were happening around me, but I was just standing there. I heard Terrence tell my mom he was gonna go after Kevon. And I saw Lawrence and Ennis on the floor trying to see if they could fix the laptop, then my mom was next to me, saying, "They're going to fix it, Jarrett. Don't worry. It's going to be okay."

It was hard to focus on what she was saying though. I looked at Caprice again, and she was looking at me like she was worried. I felt so stupid.

The whole thing was like a bad nightmare.

All I knew was I had to get away from all these people. I had to get away before I started crying or before I got so mad I started throwing things and ended up getting in trouble. I didn't know where I was gonna go, but I had to get outta there.

THIRTY-SEVEN

I KNEW MY MOM WAS FOLLOWING ME. I COULD hear the stroller. She was letting me walk about half a block ahead of her, but she was there.

I unlocked the downstairs door and went upstairs to our floor. Inside, I went right to my room without even turning on any lights or anything. Being in the dark made sense after everything that had just happened to me.

This was supposed to be, like, one of the best days of the summer. Actually of my whole life. Making that trailer was the only thing I knew how to do good. I was a big loser the rest of the time. But now, because of Kevon, everything I'd worked for was gone.

I wanted to kill him.

It took a while for Mom to come to my room, but she stayed in the doorway. I was on the top bunk, arms folded, looking straight up at the ceiling. "Are you okay?" she asked in her nice-mother voice, the one she uses with the foster kids.

But I wasn't in the mood for it, or her. "No. I'm not okay. Why would you think I was okay?"

"What Kevon did wasn't right. He ruined the Center's property and —"

"Is *that* all you're thinking about?" I screamed. "The *Center's* property? What about my trailer? What about *me*?"

"You didn't let me finish, Jarrett. Of course I'm upset about your trailer. I was looking forward to seeing it, and I was really excited for you, but —"

I sat up. "But *what*?"

Mom came into the room, closer to my bed. "Come down, Jarrett. I want to talk to you."

I sighed extra loud so she could see how much she was bothering me. But she just stood there waiting, so I didn't have a choice but to jump down. Me and her sat on the bottom bed, and after a while she said, "Is it true, what Kevon accused you of? Did you really contact his father and, what, try to get him to come back and take Kevon away?"

I thought about lying again, the way I'd lied to Kevon, but I couldn't, not to Mom. Anyway, Kevon had the evidence against me.

"Kevon wanted to go home," I said. "I heard him crying to his caseworker that —" I cut myself off. My big mouth never knew how to shut up.

"How do you know what he said to his —"

"That's not the point," I said. "Kevon wanted to go home, and I wanted my life back. He attacked me! Don't you remember that?"

"So you texted his father?"

"No, just some guy that knows his father, " I said.

"You know that was the wrong thing to do, right, Jarrett? I taught you better than that."

"I know." She was really making me feel bad. "I was wrong — but Kevon, he was wronger."

Mom gave me a look.

"I mean, he ruined my movie. He embarrassed me in front of —"

"And you embarrassed him by bringing his father to the Center. Kevon's father has a long history of mental illness. He was getting treatment, but —"

"I already know. He stopped taking his pills."

"You knew about his father, about his condition?"

I nodded. "But not till after I sent the text. Kevon never talked about his father or anything, so I found out on my own."

"Spying?"

I nodded again. "Had to. But then he told me everything last night in the cabin." I swallowed hard, not sure if I should say what I was thinking about saying next. But I had to. "Me and him talked about our fathers."

Mom actually looked surprised. "Fathers?"

"Yeah." Then, before she could change the subject, I asked her something I'd been wanting a real answer to since I was, like, three or four. "Why don't . . . ?" My voice came out kinda scratchy for some reason. "Why don't I have a father? And don't say that thing about how he wasn't ready, because that's not an answer, and I'm old enough to know the truth."

Mom stared straight ahead for a long time, and I sat there watching her face. Her eyes looked like she wasn't really here in my room anymore. She was gone.

"Okay," she said finally, taking a deep breath. "I'll tell you."

And she did. She told me. Everything. Everything I wanted to hear anyway. I mean, maybe I might have more questions and stuff later, but that night, last night, I heard everything I needed to hear. After she finished talking, it was like my head was full.

She told me all about when she came to this country when she was almost twelve years old and how she didn't really have a lot of friends because Aunt Inez never let her do anything the other kids got to do, even when she got to high school. When she went away to college in Atlanta, she was shy, and then she met that guy, the one who turned out to be my father.

"He had a lot of problems," she told me, and she had tears in her eyes. "But I fell in love with him anyway."

I knew all about love. Still, I looked down at the floor because I wasn't sure I wanted to hear all of that stuff.

"Then after three years of college," Mom said, "I came home for summer break and found out I was pregnant. With you. I didn't want him to know. I just wanted to have you and raise you in peace, without all that drama, you know? Aunt Inez told me she would help me, and she did. So I did it without him."

"Are you saying — ?"

She nodded. "I'm saying, he never knew about you, Jarrett. Never."

Like I said, that conversation had my head full. All stuffed with information and questions and confusion. My mom had lied to me my whole life. It wasn't that he hadn't been ready to be a father. He never even knew I existed.

Since we were still sitting there, and since I finally had my mom's attention, I had to say something I had been thinking about for a real long time. I said, "You know, sometimes it's like —" I shook my head. "Forget it."

"It's like what?" Mom asked. "Tell me."

I shrugged. I didn't wanna hurt her feelings or anything, but I was tired of holding everything inside. "Sometimes I feel like you care more about the babies than me. I mean, maybe when I was little you loved me more, but now — you don't even have time for me. They come first all the time."

Mom gasped. "Is that the way you really feel?" She was looking at me like it was the first time she ever saw me.

"I'm sorry," I mumbled real fast. "I didn't mean to — I shouldn't have said anything."

"No, no." Mom wiped the tears from her cheek. "I'm the one who should be sorry. I know it's hard for you, all these babies around all the time. But they need me, and — I don't know — maybe I need them, too."

I couldn't think of anything to say, so I folded my arms across my chest. I didn't wanna tell her I needed her, too, because I wasn't a baby. I could take care of myself. But still. That wasn't the point. I was her *real* kid. Why did I always have to be last?

I didn't say any of that though. Didn't have to. Mom put

her arm around me and said, "Jarrett, there's nobody in this world I love more than you."

I think I might have smiled a little bit, but only on the inside. Too much was going on in my brain, and I was still mad and tired. As a matter of fact, I was convinced I would never smile again, not till Kevon was outta my house and I had my life back again.

What was left of it anyway.

▪ ▪ ▪

It was probably an hour and a half later that Terrence came back with Kevon. I heard him and Mom talking in the kitchen. Terrence said he talked to Kevon and calmed him down. Mom said she was gonna make Kevon sleep on the couch, just so there wasn't any trouble between me and him.

If by *trouble* she meant *murder*, then she was right keeping him away from me.

A while later I heard Terrence leave, and I laid there waiting to see if Kevon was gonna show his face in my room. I was breathing hard like a panther waiting for its prey, ready to pounce in a second.

Kevon Underwood had ruined my whole life, and I wasn't gonna let him get away with it.

THIRTY-EIGHT

SEPTEMBER 4, 1:06 A.M.

A MINUTE AFTER KEVON SNEAKS INTO MY ROOM, takes his stuff, and leaves, I'm still awake, listening to his footsteps in the hall. A few seconds later they stop, and I'm thinking, *Is he gonna change his mind and stay?* Then I hear Treasure cry, just a little bit, but it's enough for me to know what he's up to.

I don't even have to think about what I do next. I'm down from my bed in a millisecond and running outta my room. If Kevon wants to take off in the middle of the night, that's okay with me. But no way am I gonna let him take Treasure. Somebody's gotta protect her.

In the hall, Kevon is putting a sweater on her. She's half crying, half sleeping, and the stroller is folded up on the floor next to them. I practically have to jump over them to get to the front door, and when I do, I block it with my body. I tell him, "I don't care where you're going, Kevon, but if you think you're taking that baby with you, you're crazier than I thought you were."

Kevon stands up with Treasure in his arms and she quiets down. "She's my sister," he says. "I can take her wherever I want."

"That's what you think." I'm so mad at him, I can't even keep my breathing normal. There's no way I'm gonna let him get past me with Treasure. She needs to stay right here. Safe with us. "Give her to me," I say, and my voice is as tough and strong as it's ever been.

Right then, Treasure starts squirming and reaching out for me. "Stop, Treasure," Kevon says, trying to hold on to her, but she doesn't stop.

"You're not taking her, Kevon. I'm serious."

Kevon glares at me, trying to intimidate me, but it's not working. I'm done letting him get to me. So me and him just stand there, face-to-face, man-to-man, for a long time.

Then he gives up. Probably he knows I'm not gonna move from the door, so he doesn't have any choice. He hands Treasure over to me and tells me, "I'm gonna find my father, and as soon as he's back on his pills, I'm coming back for her."

"That's what you think." I put my arms around Treasure to get her to calm down, but she starts crying and reaching out for Kevon. Now she wants him instead of me. She must know he's about to leave her. Babies are smart that way.

"Move!" Kevon says, like if he leaves fast enough Treasure won't notice.

So I move away from the door, but still, it takes Kevon a couple seconds to open it. He keeps looking at Treasure, like he doesn't know what to do, but finally he steps out into the hall real slow.

Treasure starts crying louder now, trying to get outta my arms and go back to Kevon. She knows something's wrong, and she's probably scared or something. If she doesn't stop crying, my mom is gonna wake up and find out what's going on.

Kevon is still standing out there in the hall. "Stop, Treasure," he whispers. "I'm gonna come back. I'm not gonna leave you here forever." He keeps talking to her, trying to calm her down, but it's not working. She doesn't want him to go.

If he leaves, she's gonna cry forever. We're never gonna hear her laugh again. I don't know why I say this, but I tell him, "You don't have to go, you know. I mean, if you wanna, you can go, but if you don't . . ."

"I have to. My dad, he needs me. You saw him."

"But Treasure, she needs you, too. Look at her. She doesn't want you to go."

Kevon looks like he wants to take her back, but no way am I giving her to him so he can try and run away with her again. "My dad," he says. "He's alone, like, for real."

I nod. "Okay, but . . ." I wanna say something else, but I can't think of anything. And before I can, he runs down the stairs. A few seconds later, the door downstairs opens and shuts. I wait to see if he's gonna change his mind and come back, but when he doesn't, I don't have a choice. I close the door and lock it, then go over to the living room window with Treasure and look outside. And I see him when he passes under one of the streetlights. He's walking real fast, like he knows exactly where he's going.

I've been waiting for this day, wanting him to leave for, like, a month, but it's real now. He's gone. And me, all I can do is stand there thinking I should do something. But what?

THIRTY-NINE

I'M STILL STANDING AT THE WINDOW HOLDING Treasure, who's falling asleep again, when I hear Mom come down the hall. "What's going on?" she asks. "Why is this stroller — ?"

"I'm in here," I say.

Mom comes into the living room. "What are you doing up? And why is Treasure . . . ?" She looks around. "Where's Kevon? Were you two boys fighting again?"

"No," I say. "Not really."

"Where is he?"

"Um." I swallow hard. What can I say? How am I supposed to tell her? "Kevon, um, he left. Ran away."

"What?" Mom screams. "Ran away? You let him leave? Oh, Lawd! Oh, God! If anything happens to that boy out there . . ." She's panicking and pacing back and forth. "How long ago did he leave?"

"Like, I don't know, five minutes, or ten."

More questions, more answers, and even more questions. Mom is going crazy. She's scared for Kevon and mad at me. I let him leave. It's my fault.

Finally, Mom gets on the phone, but she doesn't call the police like I expect her to. "It's me," she says, and then she starts crying. "I need you."

■ ■ ■

I'm on the couch, still holding Treasure, who's sleeping, when Terrence walks through the door. "I drove around the neighborhood," he says, "but I didn't see him. What happened? He just left?"

"We have to find him," Mom says. "He can't be out there by himself. Anything can happen to him."

"I know," Terrence says, putting his arms around Mom and pulling her close to him. "I know. Don't worry."

"I have to call the police," Mom says, still wrapped up in Terrence's arms. "But then the agency, they're going to take Treasure away if —"

"Shhh," Terrence says. "Let's just slow down and figure this out." It kinda looks like he doesn't wanna let her go. "We're gonna find him."

I wanna say something, but I don't know what. My mind is too crowded, confused, and I can't sort it out. I don't know what to do.

I can find Kevon. I know where he's going. But if I say anything, Terrence will go get him and bring him back here. And who knows how long he's gonna end up staying here?

Treasure changes position in my arms, but I hold her tight so she doesn't fall. If we don't find Kevon, the caseworkers will think Mom is a bad foster mother, and they'll probably come and take Treasure away. I don't think I can handle that. I mean, I know she has to leave sometime. All the foster kids do. But Treasure is different. When she leaves it's gonna hurt. I don't even wanna think about that. Not yet.

"I know where Kevon went," I say, kinda quiet so I don't wake Treasure up.

Both Mom and Terrence look over at me. "What?" Mom asks.

"I know where he went. I mean, I'm not a hundred percent sure, but —"

"Where?" Terrence asks. "Tell me."

"It's where he used to live," I say, and yeah, I know I'm doing the right thing. "I'm not sure what the name of the street is, but I followed him one time, and I can find it again. I mean, if you want me to."

"Get dressed," Mom says real fast. "Terrence, can you drive Jarrett over there?"

"Course," Terrence says. "C'mon, Jarrett. Hurry up."

Mom comes over and takes Treasure from me. Then I go to my room and put on my jeans and sneakers. I don't believe I'm about to do what I'm doing. I mean, am I really gonna go out there in the middle of the night and look for Kevon after what he did to me? Like it's my job to rescue him or something.

On the way out the door, Terrence gives Mom a kiss and tells her not to worry, that we're gonna find him. Then we go down the stairs and outside. This is the latest I've ever been outside before, but I'm not scared or anything. Terrence is with me.

■ ■ ■

All the way to Kevon's building, me and Terrence look out for Kevon, but we don't see him. But that's probably because we get kinda lost on our way there. I'm trying to remember how I got to Kevon's apartment last time, when I followed him that day, but he took so many turns and shortcuts, and it's so dark out here now, I can't help but get confused.

On one street, there are people everywhere, standing outside of bars and clubs and stuff. It's almost two o'clock in the morning, but you wouldn't know it by how many people are out here. There's a lot going on.

"Looks like them Labor Day parties are just now breaking up," Terrence says. "Folks act like they don't have to be at work in a couple hours."

All I'm thinking is, Kevon is out here somewhere. I still hate him, but that doesn't mean I want him to get hurt.

We turn off that street, onto some regular blocks with rows of two- and three-story apartments, and then I see the bodega downstairs from Kevon's apartment, the one where Paco works. "That's it," I tell Terrence. "Kevon lives right there, over that store."

Terrence parks in front of the building. "C'mon," he says, and me and him get out and go up to the door. There's no buzzer or anything on the outside of the building, but it doesn't matter. The door is busted now, so we just walk right in.

It's completely dark in the lobby, so Terrence takes out his phone and puts on the flashlight. Now I can see how bad Kevon was living. There are bags of garbage in the corner, but they got holes, so garbage is coming outta them. And somebody threw out an old mattress on the other side of the lobby. I don't know how to tell which apartment is Kevon's. Terrence points to a mailbox and shines the flashlight on it.

H. Underwood 2B.

There are only three apartments on the second floor. Me and Terrence walk down the hall real slow, trying not wake anybody up on the floor. But we don't even have to knock on the door to Kevon's apartment because there's a big, giant padlock on the outside of the door, and a sign that says

MARSHAL'S LEGAL POSSESSION

The Landlord Has Legal Possession of These Premises Pursuant to Warrant of Civil Court

"What does that mean?" I whisper to Terrence.

"It means nobody was paying the rent, so the landlord locked them out till they pay up. C'mon. He ain't in there."

"Where is he, then?"

Terrence shakes his head. "We gotta go look for him."

■ ■ ■

Back in the car, we sit there for a little while, waiting to see if Kevon shows up. Maybe we got there before he did. Maybe he doesn't even know they locked him outta his apartment yet.

But he doesn't show up, and after a while, Terrence turns on the engine and we start to drive around, real slow, just circling the neighborhood, one block at a time.

"I don't even know why I'm looking for him," I say, "I mean, after what he did to me."

"Y'all both did the wrong thing," Terrence says.

"I know, but —" Terrence doesn't understand. Kevon embarrassed me in front of everybody at the Center.

And I did the same thing to him.

I wish it was easier to make him worse than me.

I look out my window. More buildings. More empty streets. Then we turn another corner and everything changes. There are, like, four police cars out there with their lights flashing, and two ambulances. There are crowds of people standing around on the sidewalk. Something bad definitely happened here.

My heart pumps so hard, I can practically hear it. "You think — ?"

"Let's go see what's up." Terrence pulls up to the curb and puts the car in park. We get out and walk over to where everybody is standing. Even before we get there, I know for a fact somebody got shot because I hear people talking, saying stuff about guns and this neighborhood and how the police never come around here till after it's over.

Terrence goes up to one of the cops. "Excuse me," he says. "My son and me, we're looking for a boy, twelve years old." He turns to me. "What was he wearing, Jarrett?"

"I don't know. Like jeans and a T-shirt or something." I know I'm not helping anybody, but it's hard to think after Terrence calls me his son.

Terrence turns back to the cop. "Was it a kid that was — ?"

"No, sir. Two men got shot inside this club."

Me and Terrence look at each other. I know people are hurt, but at least it's not Kevon. He's still out here somewhere.

■ ■ ■

After driving around for a long, long time, going around the whole neighborhood real slow, up and down the streets, I'm thinking, *Where is he already?* It's like he disappeared.

Just when I'm about to give up, Terrence pulls up to a red light and right there, outta my window, I see him. Kevon. He's sitting on a bench inside a bus shelter. His big, ugly army bag is on the bench next to him.

"Kevon!" I yell outta the window. "Kevon!"

He looks up, sees me, and doesn't move. He just sits there.

Terrence pulls over to park, and I jump outta the car and run over to Kevon. "What's the matter with you?" I ask him. "We've been looking for you, like, forever."

"I didn't ask you to find me."

"Just come on."

He shakes his head. "I have to find my father. I told you."

I sit down next to him. "You're not gonna find him tonight. It's dark and —"

"I'm gonna wait till it's morning."

Terrence comes over, and now me and him are trying to get Kevon to come back with us. But Kevon is like one of those videos that plays over and over in a loop. All he keeps saying is how much his father needs him.

Terrence sits down on the other side of Kevon. "Look, man," he says. "I know you wanna help your father, but he needs professional help. In a hospital."

Kevon doesn't say anything.

"We're gonna find him," Terrence says. "But when we do, we need to find a place where he can go for a while, you know, to get cleaned up and back on his medication. I'm gonna help, okay?"

Kevon looks sad and kinda lost. He doesn't even look twelve anymore. He looks younger than me. Finally, he says, "Fine." Then he looks around and asks, "Now what am I supposed to do?"

I'm not sure who he's talking to, me or Terrence, but I'm so tired I just say, "You're supposed to come back to my house, stupid."

"You're stupid," he says.

"I didn't run away in the middle of the night."

"You too scared to run away."

Terrence stands up over both of us and points his finger at us. "Look," he says. "Y'all gotta figure out how to get along, you hear me? All this childish fighting, y'all gotta let that go. You know what I'm saying?"

I don't need to hear this. What does Terrence think I'm

gonna do, fight with Kevon forever? He needs to give me more credit than that.

Anyway, Kevon doesn't even have anywhere else to go. What did he think I was gonna do when we found him? Leave him out here in the middle of the night by himself? I don't hate him that much.

Me and Kevon nod, then follow Terrence back to the car. And for some reason me and him both get in the backseat, even though Mom isn't there to sit in the front. But I'm too tired to move. I just wanna get home already.

FORTY

THE SECOND ALL THREE OF US WALK INTO THE house, Mom starts crying, which doesn't even make any sense because we're back now and everybody's okay. She wraps her arms around Kevon first and says, "Oh, my goodness. I'm so relieved you're okay. You scared me to death."

"I know," Kevon says.

"You know I love you, right?" Mom asks.

"Yeah, I know." Kevon hugs her tighter, and for a while me and Terrence just stand there watching them. Mom's hugging him the way she hugs the babies. She never even hugs me like that anymore. But I don't need her to. Maybe Kevon does.

I start to walk into the living room, but before I get too far, Mom lets go of Kevon and hugs me the exact same way. "We never could have found him if it wasn't for you."

"It was easy," I say. I'm so tight in her arms now, but I can't say it doesn't feel good.

When Mom finally lets me go, she tells me and Kevon to wash up and get back in bed. "We have a big day tomorrow," she says. "Shopping for school clothes and —"

"New sneakers?" I ask.

She laughs. "Yes, new sneakers, for both of you."

"Yes!" Kevon says, and he actually smiles for the first time all night.

"And new underwear and socks and school supplies." Mom is back in mom mode now. "Oh, yeah, I have to call Central Boys first thing to find out if there's room for you, Kevon. And to let Mr. Johnson know how excited you are to be going there, Jarrett."

"Ugh." I sigh. There is no getting outta any of this. I'm gonna start at Central Boys on Wednesday.

Summer is over.

"Go on, boys. Get to sleep. I need to talk to Terrence." Then, before me and Kevon can even go down the hall, Mom puts her arms around Terrence's shoulders. She doesn't hug him like she hugged us. She kisses him. Just like they used to before they broke up. It's like they're forgetting me and Kevon are standing there.

I whisper to Kevon, "Let's get outta here."

"I'm right behind you."

Me and him practically run down the hall to our room just so we don't have to see any more kissing. I mean, nobody should have to witness that kinda thing.

Kevon drops his army bag on the floor by the bed. Then he sits on the bed and stares straight ahead like he's in a trance.

"You tired?" I ask him, even though I already know the answer.

"Yeah. You?"

"Dead." I climb up on my bed without even changing back

into the sweatpants I was sleeping in before. Too tired. I lay my head on the pillow and close my eyes, but there's no way I can sleep. Not after everything that happened tonight.

Kevon gets up and turns off the light, and for, like, five minutes we're quiet. Then I hear Mom laughing in the living room. Terrence is still here. And they're not arguing or anything.

"You up?" I ask Kevon.

"Yeah, I can't sleep."

"Me neither."

"You think they're gonna get back together?" Kevon asks me.

"I don't know. Yeah, probably. I mean, I hope so."

"Me, too."

Then Kevon is quiet again.

"Terrence is gonna help you find your father," I tell him. "Don't worry."

"I'm trying not to."

I flip over onto my back, then turn to my side. My brain is all over the place, and I can't stop thinking about everything. Kevon is back and so is Terrence. But that doesn't fix everything. Not for me. I'm still in sixth grade, and I don't know how the other guys are gonna treat me. Or Caprice. I don't know if I'm ever gonna be able to tell her how I feel about her, that I want her to be my girlfriend, not just a friend.

And now I gotta go to a different school, and Kevon will probably end up there with me. It's kinda like I got a brother or something.

And a sister.

I sit up on the bed. "I give up. You think my mom will let us watch a monster movie or something?"

"Let's go see." Kevon is off his bed before I can jump down off mine. "But not that movie we saw last time. It was so dumb."

"Human heads were rolling down the street," I remind him. "How can something like that be dumb?"

"It just was."

I follow him down the hall, shaking my head. I'm not sure how long Kevon is gonna be staying with us. But he has a lot to learn.

ABOUT THE AUTHOR

Coe Booth is the author of the YA novels *Tyrell* (winner of the Los Angeles Times Book Prize), *Kendra,* and *Bronxwood.* She was born in the Bronx and still lives there. This is her first book for younger readers.